SUMMER ROSE

SUMMER ROSE

Carole Dean

Chivers Press   •   G.K. Hall & Co.
Bath, England   Waterville, Maine USA

This Large Print edition is published by Chivers Press, England, and by G.K. Hall & Co., USA.

Published in 2001 in the U.K. by arrangement with the Author c/o Dorie Simmonds.

Published in 2001 in the U.S. by arrangement with Kensington Books, an imprint of Kensington Publishing Corp.

U.K. Hardcover ISBN 0-7540-4562-5 (Chivers Large Print)
U.K. Softcover ISBN 0-7540-4563-3 (Camden Large Print)
U.S. Softcover ISBN 0-7838-9477-5 (Nightingale Series Edition)

The text of this Large Print edition is unabridged.
Other aspects of the book may vary from the original edition.

Set in 16 pt. New Times Roman.

Printed in Great Britain on acid-free paper.

British Library Cataloguing in Publication Data available

Library of Congress Cataloging-in-Publication Data

Dean, Carole.
    Summer rose / Carole Dean.
        p.   cm.
    ISBN 0-7838-9477-5 (lg. print : sc : alk. paper)
    1. Large type books. I. Title.
    PS3554.E14 S86 2001
    813'.54—dc21   2001024202

For Vera, Doddie, and Nat, the very best of friends.
There can never be too many August weekends.

And for Cody, who waits for me by the Rainbow Bridge.

CHAPTER ONE

'Rosaleen Fiona O'Hanlon, you're certifiable.'

Rosie grinned but didn't look away from her computer screen. 'Must be bad if you're bringing the full weight of my Celtic heritage to bear, Jonesy. What's the problem?'

'You're broke. Flatter than a cheap perm.'

'Uh-huh.' Using her foot, Rosie rubbed the belly of the Irish wolfhound sprawled at her feet. He stretched and groaned his appreciation.

'You have the income of a poet and you're spending like Ivana.'

Rosie raised her eyebrows and scanned her modest home office, which she affectionately called Litter Hill. Ivana wouldn't use it for shoe storage. Still, it was Rosie's and it was home. She loved it. And so did Font, the one hundred and twenty pound heap of canine currently taking up all unused floor space.

'Well, keep it to yourself, okay?' She squinted at the screen, for now jacked up on a wooden tomato crate, and pushed her glasses up her nose. 'Wouldn't want it on my head if bank stocks plummet.'

'I'm surprised your bank hasn't already,' Jonesy said, leaning back in her chair and crossing her arms. 'You're not taking this seriously, you know.'

'You're serious enough for both of us. And I want to get this section done before noon. Hennessy's coming by with more projects.' She shoved her hair back and off her forehead, but it did no good. Masses of screeching red hair, wildly curly, swirled around her face and brushed against her skin. Skin that was the site of an ongoing war for territory between creamy alabaster and golden freckles. For now, it being late spring, the alabaster was winning.

A distinct 'ahem' brought Rosie's attention back to her longtime friend and accountant. Resigned to a lecture, she rotated her upper body to face a still glaring Jonesy.

'Okay, I give up. Why am I certifiable?'

'You've lost a lot of time—and money—as a result of your surgery and convalescence. The result being these.' She waved a hand over the table she'd been working on. It was piled high with unpaid bills. 'As a technical writer, you work by the hour, right?'

'Right.'

'And MooreWrite wants to give you more work, right?'

'Right again.' Rosie would have nodded, but the neck brace she was wearing precluded so much as a dip of her chin. She ran her index finger between it and her itchy neck. Damn thing!

'But instead of taking the more lucrative work to make up for lost time, you're writing

2

love letters for the dating impaired for pennies a pop.'

'Hey, that's not fair. My clients—'

'Humph!'

Rosie gave her a stern look. 'I repeat, my *clients* are not, as you so callously put it, "dating impaired". If they were, they wouldn't have anyone to write to, would they?'

'*Cyrano Inc.* is an idea gone wrong. It's been over a month now and you have nothing to show for it. Your skills would be better employed elsewhere. Logic—and your current financial pickle—says your time should go to the highest bidder. And that, dear heart, is MooreWrite Technical Inc. Economics, pure and simple.' Jonesy clamped her lips firmly together and gave her a hard stare.

Rosie frowned. Jonesy was right, but it didn't matter. *Cyrano Inc.* might have started on a whim, but it had turned out to be oddly fulfilling. Telling someone—anyone—they were loved and desired was a ton more interesting than writing, 'If all else fails, check your power source. You may have neglected to plug in.'

And writing the letters gave her hope.

In the hospital, she'd become acutely aware someone was missing from her bedside crowd of friends and colleagues—a very special someone. Okay, maybe it had been just post-op blues, but it had made her think about what she wanted from life. Or to be exact, *who* she

3

wanted from life.

At twenty-eight, after what seemed a lifetime of trial-and-error dating, she'd struck out. Maybe writing anonymous love letters was a bit off-the-wall, but at least her customers didn't have to check their wiring. They were already connected, which was more than could be said for her. *That* was about to change—and soon.

Rosie had an agenda.

She was going to find her special someone, and nothing was going to stand in her way. For once she was going to listen to her mother. She could hear her now: 'When you really want something, Rosaleen, visualize it clearly, develop a practical plan, then do the work necessary to get it.'

Of course, she'd been talking about financial and career success at the time—when wasn't she?—but what the heck, the advice was still good, and, besides, the definition of success, and career, for that matter, was definitely subjective. Much as her mother would like it to be otherwise, Rosie didn't want a trendy career, she wanted the perfect man. And when this Meccano set came off her neck, she was going to get him.

'And another thing,' Jonesy wasn't finished.

Rosie groaned.

'Sell this place. The mortgage is killing you.'

'But it's doing wonders for the Font.' Rosie nudged the inert mound of dog with her toe.

4

He didn't move. 'He's like a pup since we moved here.'

Jonesy looked skyward and did that funny thing with her lips, which involved pursing and lip chewing while drawing in a deep breath. Rosie tried not to grin.

'So, you're telling me you *won't* stop wasting your time on *Cyrano*, you *won't* sell this money pit of a farmhouse, and you *won't* take more contracts from MooreWrite?'

'Right. On two out of three.'

Jonesy's gaze didn't waver.

'I will—read my lips, Jonesy—I *will* take on more work from MooreWrite. Hennessy says they've just signed a contract to update their computer-training manuals. If I get a piece of that project, it'll see me through to the next millennium—or make my next mortgage payment. Whichever comes first.' She arched her brows. 'Happy now?'

Jonesy's stern expression turned to worry. 'Burning the midnight oil isn't the answer, Rosie. It's too soon after your surgery. What you need to do is prioritize—'

'Ugh, I hate that word. It sounds like something involving rubber gloves and suction.'

Jonesy threw up her hands. 'I quit. I just quit.'

'Good. Then I can get back to work.' She pointed to her computer. 'This is for MooreWrite, after all. Real top-dollar stuff,

5

Jonesy. Honestly.'

Jonesy snapped her laptop closed. 'Have them send the cash directly to the nearest poorhouse. Maybe they'll give you an early-bird discount if you book your room in advance.'

Rosie laughed. 'You're damn sharp for a bean counter, you know that? Now go, already, and let me get to work.'

Jonesy stood and gathered up her computer and papers. That done, she looked down at Rosie. 'How's the back, anyway? Better?'

'Much. It won't be long until this—' she touched the metal brace encasing her neck '—gets recycled into a plant stand. The doctor says from then on, back flips and somersaults are definitely out, but other than that, life returns to normal.'

'Normal, huh?' Jonesy gave her a narrow look. 'I wonder if your doctor has any idea what that word means applied to you.'

Rosie's grin widened. 'Go, Jonesy. Go! Thanks for the advice. I really will try to— what was that word again?'

'Prioritize?' Jonesy raised a skeptical brow.

'Right.'

Jonesy headed to the door.

'And Jonesy?' Rosie called, still smiling.

She turned.

'Your check is in the mail.'

*   *   *

Kent Summerton picked up the stack of mail on his desk and fanned through it impatiently. He pulled one letter out, cursed under his breath, and shoved it in his desk drawer. He turned another over in his hand and looked at the return address. No luck.

He tossed the whole stack back on his desk and ran a hand along the nape of his neck, where the tendons were tight as guy wires.

He wasn't surprised. Responding to the stupid ad had yielded exactly the results he'd expected. Zip. A waste of stationery. *Cyrano Inc.* was probably one more one-ad brainchild of some hare-brained entrepreneur. He cursed again and massaged his neck muscles. He was beat, wrung out. He was thirty-two and felt like a hundred. Right now, if he had a choice between hot, mind-numbing sex and eight hours in the sack alone, alone would win. Not that he had time for either sleep or sex.

'Kent, can I see you a minute?'

Dressed in her usual dark suit and silk blouse, his assistant, Marlene Grant, waited just inside his open office door, holding a file and a notebook.

He admired Marlene. On the job. Too bad he couldn't admire her in a more intimate way. Puzzling, because she was ambitious, organized, and focused—all traits he respected in a woman—and she gave off all the right signals. Trouble was he had another woman on his mind, and he couldn't shake her loose. She was fast becoming an obsession.

'If you're busy, I'll come back later,' Marlene said.

He'd have to think about his 'obsession' later. Right now, he had a business to run. He dropped the mail on the desk and waved her in. 'Have a seat.'

Still standing, he leaned to open his file drawer. 'While you're here, we can review the food and beverage stats.' Right about now, chewing a bundle of hay held more appeal, but it had to be done, and he was the only one around to do it.

She strode in, sat in the chair facing his desk, and crossed her legs. Kent's gaze ricocheted off them on its way to the files he was pulling from his drawer. Even her legs looked organized. Or maybe thirty-two marked the beginning of his sexual decline. On that dreary thought, he took his chair.

'Before the stats, could we discuss this proposal for a computerized tee system? It looks like a piece of junk to me, but Con just said he thinks it's a great idea.' She put a thick file on his desk and shoved it toward him.

'Con's here?' Kent's head jerked up in time to catch Marlene's businesslike nod. Conrad York was his business partner—or so their partnership agreement said. Kent was starting to wonder. Lately, Con had taken to doing one hell of a disappearing act. Hadn't been around for a week. But today Kent had him. Just a blip on his sonar, maybe—but it was enough. 'Marlene, could this meeting wait?'

She stood. 'I'll come back at three.' Her words dripped annoyance.

'Thanks.' Kent was out the door and at the pro shop in seconds. Too late. Con was already on the third tee.

*   *   *

Rosie picked up the mail in the front hall before sinking gratefully into the big recliner by the fireplace. She rested her armored neck on the chair back and looked out over her fenced backyard. Beyond the fence lay twenty acres of pastoral heaven, a blurred mosaic of dandelions, clover, and untamed grass. Her neighbor's five cows viewed it more practically—as a salad—and were dining in fine style in the second pasture. The yard, the pasture, the crop of dandelions were all hers, and she loved them passionately.

Sell the place, Jonesy had said. *Not in this lifetime, my dear friend.* Rosaleen Fiona O'Hanlon intended to raise her children in this house. All she needed was the right man. She closed her eyes.

In the midst of a fantasy involving a hot-blooded Mr. Right intent on an afternoon sexcapade which included whipped cream, champagne, and a braceless Rosie, her

9

bloodless computer burped a reminder to get back to work.

'Just a minute,' she yelled. 'I'm opening the mail.'

She leafed through the windowed envelopes. Rosie figured if her name was spelled wrong, it was a solicitation; if it was spelled right, it was a bill. Both she saved for last or for never. She smiled. Who said she couldn't prioritize? After sorting, two pieces remained: a letter from Mary Poppins, the code name for one of her *Cyrano* customers, and a large envelope from *The Morning Times* which she knew would be responses to her most recent ad.

She tore it open and three letters fell out.

Not enough, Rosie girl, not nearly enough. The dismal thought neither dulled her curiosity nor dimmed her enthusiasm. The return address for one of the letters was Beachline Resort. She knew the place, a small but classy hotel with a golf course and a series of well-appointed cabins along a bluff not far from downtown Victoria, and maybe fifteen miles south of her own property. The breath-stopping views attracted anyone with money enough to afford them. Rosie had lunched there with a few of the MooreWrite people when she'd signed her contract with them, well over a year ago.

She tore open the letter.

Dear Mr./Ms. Cyrano:
I read your ad in The Morning Times and
would like to discuss same. Please call or write
to arrange an appointment with me in my
office at your earliest convenience. A prompt
reply would be appreciated.
Thanking you, I remain,

Yours truly,
K.L. Summerton
General Manager

Rosie whistled softly. Definitely a buttoned-down type—and she wasn't thinking shirt collars. She shuddered. Ambitious suits weren't her style. But, running her ad in the financial pages, she should have expected this type of response, and there was always the chance *Mr. Button-Down* would pay well. As for meeting him in his office, it wasn't going to happen. She wouldn't be driving until her neck brace was in the nearest dumpster.

She glanced at the other responses; a fancy brochure from a company offering shared office space downtown, and a job application from an unemployed poet. Jonesy would *love* that. She grinned and pushed herself up from the chair.

'Okay, Mr. Button-Down, you're up,' she announced.

Back in her office, she picked up her receiver and keyed the number from the letterhead.

11

'Beachline Resort.' A woman's friendly voice smiled down the line. 'May I help you?'

'Mr. Summerton, please.' Rosie waited to the tune of a Strauss waltz. She was swaying to it and trying to identify it when a man's deep voice broke the rhythm.

'Kent Summerton here,' he said, as if clipping the words from a dry branch. His tone was authoritative and had the immediate effect of making her square her shoulders.

'Mr. Summerton. I'm Rosie O'Hanlon, from *Cyrano Inc.* You asked that I call to arrange an appointment and I—'

'Tomorrow morning would be good for me. This afternoon would be even better,' he said, his voice brusque to the point of rudeness.

Rosie held the receiver in front of her, frowned at it, and returned it to her ear. *Definitely* a button-down. 'I don't make house calls, Mr. Summerton. I do business by e-mail, snailmail, fax, or telephone.'

'This isn't business as usual. Your name again?'

'Rosie O'Hanlon.'

'Miss, Mrs., or Ms.?' he asked, as if he were about to put a tick in a box.

Rosie considered telling him to use her first name but decided against it. 'Miss,' she said in as formal a tone as she could muster.

'As I was saying, Miss O'Hanlon, this is not business as usual. And even if I'm miles off track here, I figure it's worth a shot.'

12

'I'm sorry, I don't follow you.' What in heaven's name was the man talking about?

'What I'm trying to say is that I've been receiving letters from a woman named Gardenia. I'd like to know if she used your love letter service.'

Rosie didn't hesitate. 'My business is confidential. You'll have to ask your woman friend if she—'

'I don't *have* a woman friend—at least not in the sense you mean—so I can't ask. I have no idea who this Gardenia person is. That's why I'm talking to you, Miss O'Hanlon.'

CHAPTER TWO

'Oh.' Rosie let the word seep through the line while she gathered her thoughts. 'You mean they're anonymous letters?' she finally added, stating the obvious.

'You got it in one.'

'Oh,' she repeated, her feet firmly on shaky ground. She'd never figured on something like this. Still, there was no reason to believe someone using her service had initiated the letters. No reason at all.

'Is that the extent of your comments? "Oh?"' he drawled.

Snide, she decided. The man was definitely snide. 'I was thinking—'

13

'Sorry it's so difficult for you.'

The roots of her red hair took fire. 'Look, why don't you get a prescription for courtesy pills, take a leave of absence from that high-stress job of yours, and call me when you've rejoined the human race. Good-bye, Mr. Summerton.' She hung up, teed off, but smugly pleased with herself.

She was even more pleased when she realized he couldn't call her back because she hadn't left her number. She couldn't believe how rude the man was. Pompous ass.

Halfway back to her desk, the phone rang in her hand. She pushed the talk button and lifted it to her ear.

'How did you know I've got a high-stress job?' he asked without preliminaries.

'How did *you* get this number?'

'Ever hear of call display?'

While Rosie inwardly cursed modern technology, he went on. 'Look, I'm sorry I was abrupt, but I'm on a tight schedule, and I don't have time for this Gardenia business. I'm damned fed up with being written to by a crazy woman—'

'You're sure it's a woman? Maybe it's a deranged bear with a thorn in its paw looking for a soul mate.'

Silence.

'Okay,' he said. 'Let's say I deserved that. Can we start from the beginning?'

'We can, but my guess is we'll end up at the

14

same place. I tried to tell you, Mr.—what was your name again?' She knew exactly what his name was.

He sighed into the phone. 'Summerton.'

'As I tried to tell you, Mr. Summerton, I think it's unreasonable of you to assume the letters came from *Cyrano*. Lots of people write love letters.'

'Not like these. They have a . . . professional touch. And when I caught your ad in the morning paper, I thought—Hell, I don't know what I thought. I told you it's a long shot.'

'Well, start shooting in another direction because—'

'Hold on a minute.'

She heard paper rustling.

'Tiger. I adore you, by now you must know that. But do you know my dreams are crowded with your image, colored by the jade of your restless, loving eyes? At night, when you come to me, you fill my heart, my mind. You are so real, so powerful I can feel your hard—' He stopped as suddenly as he'd began. 'Recognize it?'

Rosie's heart bumped down her ribs like a gutter-born bowling ball, and landed solidly in her stomach. She pulled a coil of hair loose and tugged on it. Her mom always said that she did this when she wanted a direct route to the logical part of her brain. If that were true, she'd picked the wrong strands. This hair seemed to be rooted in the what-do-I-do-now

15

section. No help at all. No doubt about it, he had read her words.

When she didn't answer, he added in painfully patient tones. 'Simple question, Miss O'Hanlon. Did you write that, or didn't you?'

'I'm thinking.'

The man was a quick study. This time he left her to it.

She pondered her situation. Summerton was receiving unsolicited love letters. Her face warmed. Very explicit love letters. The woman who'd ordered them wasn't engaged to 'Tiger,' as she'd claimed, and because of her lie, Rosaleen Fiona O'Hanlon was in the business of writing junk mail.

'Yes. I wrote it,' she grumped, figuring she'd owed him that much.

'Great! Just tell me who you wrote it for; I'll contact her and put an end to it.'

'I can't do that.'

She heard him inhale his frustration and let it out on a long breath. 'Look, I respect your need to protect your customer's confidentiality, but you've got to understand my position here. I didn't ask for these letters, and I want them stopped. Is that clear?'

It was clear the man was a horse's tail-flicking backside. 'I can't tell you, because I don't know.'

'Excuse me?' He sounded confused.

'She didn't give me her real name.'

'I see. Her telephone number, then.'

16

'Sorry. She always called me.'

'Address?' He was beginning to sound wistful.

'Nope. She phoned me to order the letters—for her fiancé, she said—and I mailed them to a box number at the main post office.'

'What about payment? She must have sent you a check or money order.' He was all business again. Rosie imagined him reaching for a pen and paper, a nice clean piece of paper from one of those little plastic boxes sitting just so on a big shiny desk. He probably had one of those magnet things for his paper clips, too. And at least a five-tray file stacker.

'Are you there?' he asked finally.

'She made a one-time cash deposit to my account. It was enough for—' she stopped and, anticipating his reaction, grimaced '—fifty-two letters. That's what she wanted. I've already written them.'

'Fifty-two . . .' he repeated, sounding awed. Silence spilled down the line. 'Then I'm stuck,' he finally said, his voice low. 'I didn't want to involve the police in this, but—'

'Police? Why would you do that?' Rosie instantly imagined a dozen uniformed police clomping around her office, rummaging her files. The picture was irksome.

'Being stalked is not my idea of a good time, Miss O'Hanlon.'

'I wrote those letters, remember? And you're hardly being stalked. In danger of being

17

flattered to death, maybe. But stalked? I don't think so.'

'Not yet, perhaps. But my guess is this is how it starts, a few letters, then phone calls, and the next thing you know, Gardenia is peering in my bedroom window.'

He had a point, but she still didn't like the idea of a herd of detectives stumping through her house. She decided to head them off. 'I've got an idea. Interested?' Actually she had a half-baked notion, but it was better than zilch.

'Given that I'm fresh out? Absolutely, but— hold on a minute. I've got a call on the other line.'

Click. One minute. Two. He was back.

'Look, I've got to go. I've wasted too much time on this call, as it is. Would you reconsider coming to my office . . . say, tomorrow around eleven? We can talk about your idea then.'

'Sorry, you'll have to come here.' She didn't bother to explain about the neck brace and her temporary inability to drive.

'Fine.' He spit the word out as if it were a bad nut, but he didn't argue. 'Give me directions.'

She gave him her address, told him to come at noon, and hung up. Rosie studied the phone a minute before replacing it on charge. She wasn't looking forward to meeting Summerton—but she did have a responsibility to help him sort out his problem. As for Gardenia, the poor fool, she must be on

18

desperation's sharpest edge. Why else would she want to communicate with a corporate type who probably needed a crowbar to get out of his shirts?

⊮   ⊁   ⊥

Kent glared at his recradled phone. He didn't have time for this cat-and-mouse game. He glanced at the mountain of work on his desk and let out a harsh breath. He didn't have any time at all.

And he wasn't sure Rosie O'Hanlon was being straight with him, but he planned to find out.

When the unwanted letters first started coming, he'd ignored them, but as the prose grew more personal, and a hell of lot more torrid—thanks to O'Hanlon's over-sexed keyboard—he'd decided to do something. He hated wasting valuable time on some fixated fruitcake, but the letters had to be checked out. He hadn't bothered to tell this woman that he'd already contacted the police, and all he'd got for the effort was a wink and a nudge. Call them, they'd said, if the problem escalated. No damn help at all.

*   *   *

The clock struck noon and the doorbell rang. Rosie rolled her eyes. No doubt it was

19

Summerton. He *would* be right on time. She glanced down at Font, who briefly lifted his great head from the pillow she'd put down for him this morning. The lift said, 'Do you want me to do anything? Bark? Growl?' When he received no instructions, his head crashed back onto the pillow.

She ran a finger under the edge of her brace in the gesture of a man loosening a tight collar. Might as well get this over with. She drummed up a facsimile smile, walked to the door, and opened it wide.

The smile started a slow chinward slide. She caught it just before it attained full gape status. For the first time, she was glad of the unsightly contraption wreathing her neck. Without it her jaw would have thudded to her chest bone.

Kent Summerton was major hot. A perfect six feet, thick mahogany-colored hair with honey streaks, bleached by either a kind-hearted sun or a team of professional color consultants—her money was on the sun—and eyes the color of a forest in twilight. A misty, mysterious green, they were darkly lashed and directly, disconcertingly focused on her.

As she surfaced from her momentary stupor, she became aware he was speaking to—and scowling at—her.

He didn't appear to have mastered the basic introductory smile. His lips were ruler straight, his jaw square and rigidly composed. Rosie had the impression if he ever smiled fully, he'd black out from the effort. Maybe, but he was definitely top-grade eye candy. Looking at him, she had a sudden wave of empathy for the poor, besotted Gardenia.

'Miss O'Hanlon?' He bent his head, gave her a puzzled look, then slowly raised his silky, dark eyebrows. She couldn't tell what he was questioning: her hearing, her sanity, or her IQ.

She managed to twist up another smile, one wide enough to sell toothpaste, and bright enough to conceal stupefaction. 'Uh-huh. That's me. And you're Kent Summerton, of course. Come in, please.'

He nodded and stepped in. The subtle scent of his aftershave trailed him. Rosie leaned on the door, closed her eyes, and inhaled—deep. Clean, sharp, and woodsy. Lord, but she loved it when a man smelled as good as he looked. She had a sudden image of him standing in front of a mirror, splashing his jaw with aftershave, grimacing the way men do when the astringent bites their freshly shaven skin.

He took a few steps into the house and turned to face her. Surprisingly, he wasn't wearing either a suit or the button-down collar she'd been expecting. He wore gray slacks and a black golf shirt. Its soft cotton molded over his chest, draped easily over his lean torso, then disappeared under the belted waistband of his pants. Her admiration of his much-too admirable pecs led her gaze to the gold Beachline logo on his shirt, reminding her

21

what he was here for.

Business, Rosie. Think about business. She stepped away from the door, only slightly off balance.

He looked down at her, which wasn't hard. Rosie's sock height was five-three.

'Accident.' He nodded at her brace.

'Service and repair on a couple of discs. It'll be off soon. This way,' she said. He followed her lead, stepping casually over the swath of Irish wolfhound forming a roadblock at the entrance to her living room.

'Please sit down.' She indicated her recliner. 'Can I get you a coffee?'

As he sank into her most comfortable chair, he looked decidedly uncomfortable. 'No, thanks, anyway. I don't have much time.' He glanced at Font. 'Nice dog. I have a female. Same breed.'

'You have a dog?' she blurted.

He frowned.

'I guess you don't look like a dog kind of guy,' she added awkwardly. She'd have guessed the closest thing to a pet a man like Summerton would have would be an alligator briefcase.

'What kind of "guy" do I look like?'

Rosie opened her mouth and closed it, thereby giving it a whole new experience. No need to tell him she couldn't see him and a clump of dog hair sharing the same universe.

'Like a busy one, Mr. Summerton. Shall we

22

get on—'

'Kent. And Rosie, if that's okay. Considering the letters you wrote me, I think we can dispense with surnames.' He leaned back in the chair and studied her, fixing his gaze on her mouth with enough intensity to smudge her lipstick.

Her heart got all skittery. Untrustworthy thing!

'I didn't write you,' she protested. 'I mean, uh, not for myself. You know that. And I had no idea the woman was lying to me. No idea she wasn't writing to the man she loved and was planning to marry. Those letters were strictly business.'

'You're in a strange business, Rosie O'Hanlon.' He tilted his head and gave her a thoughtful look. 'And, judging from your letters, you've got one hell of an imagination. Or do you draw from first hand experience?' His voice was low, husky, and his gaze never wavered.

Her protest flopped over on its back and died somewhere deep in her throat as her face warmed to fuchsia. This time it was easy to keep her mouth shut. Temporarily, at least, she was at a loss for words. How could a man look so good, smell so good, and still be obnoxious?

'Do you actually make a living writing love letters?' he asked, his tone implying the activity was a link short of performing live sex

23

for a sailor's stag.

'No. Most of my cash comes from writing smut on bus station washrooms.' She smiled broadly and took control. 'But a girl's gotta eat.'

'Okay, okay. Sorry.'

He didn't look it, but she forgave him because of his aftershave.

'Actually, the letters are a sideline,' she conceded. 'I'm a technical writer for MooreWrite Inc. And I'm truly sorry about the letters you've been getting . . . Kent, but I think I know a way to stop them.'

'I thought you said she'd bought fifty-two, and that you'd already written and sent them to her?'

'Well, yes, that's true, but—'

'Is that your real hair color?' he asked suddenly.

'Excuse me?' She automatically raised a hand to touch her crowning headache. It had woken up with an attitude this morning. Rosie had accepted long ago that her hair had a life of its own. Somedays, she left it to wander. This was one of those days.

'I asked if that's your natural hair color?'

'You think I'd pay for this?' She wondered if all the man's neurons were firing. And she wasn't too crazy about the way he was studying her, either. Feature by feature, as if he were committing her to memory. His scrutiny made her stomach rickety.

24

He paused, then dipped his chin. 'I like it,' he said finally.

She wasn't sure he was saying it to her or himself. She stared at him through her glasses and blinked. Having a conversation with Kent Summerton was like navigating a maze with a bag over your head. Come to think of it, the idea of being stuck in a maze with this man wouldn't be too hard to take.

Back to business, Rosie!

'Do you think we could leave the subject of my hair and talk about your problem now?' She fervently wished he'd quit staring at her. Those green eyes of his were doing the most outrageous things to her nervous system, which was none too reliable in the first place.

He continued to stare until she waved a hand in front of his face. 'Mr. Summerton? Kent. Are you okay?'

'Huh?' He gave her a vacant look. 'Oh . . . yeah, the letters.'

Rosie tapped her index finger against her chin and waited for him to dredge up what wits he had. How sad. For a guy so good to look at, he had a regrettably short attention span.

He leaned forward then, rested his elbows on his knees, and riveted his smoky gaze to hers. 'Tell me your plan, Rosie. I can't wait to hear it.'

CHAPTER THREE

Kent couldn't take his eyes off her. Rosie O'Hanlon was the glowingest woman he'd ever met. It was as though he were looking into a prism; a brilliant tumble of red hair, bright lively blue eyes framed with auburn lashes, and the whitest, smoothest skin he'd ever seen, spattered with golden freckles. Add to that she had on green jeans and a sweater—he briefly closed his eyes against the glare—in a pink strong enough to cure blindness. Then there were the oversize glasses, sort of a marine blue, that she kept pushing up a nose that looked too delicate to even hold the things: One arm on the glasses had a piece of wire holding it to the frame. He glanced at her feet. Checkered black and white socks—no shoes.

He blinked and forced his gaze back to her face. Was that a mole on her cheek, just below her right eye, or was it an enlarged freckle?

'. . . not sure it will work, of course. But we can give it a try. What do you think?'

He tore his brain from the mole/freckle question and caught her puzzled gaze. He had no idea what she was saying.

'Could I have a glass of water, please?' If he'd been wearing a tie he'd have loosened it. He wasn't just warm, he was stunned by his over-the-top reaction to a woman who

26

probably kept a stash of Mickey Mouse hats in her closet. Freckles. He'd never cared for freckles. Now he couldn't help wondering how much body surface they actually covered.

Yeah, he was warm all right.

She gave him a thoughtful look, then let out a breath. 'Sure. Just a minute.' She got up from the sofa and headed through a door he assumed led to the kitchen.

Kent leaned back against the big soft chair, closed his eyes and breathed deeply. He was tense. Overtired. That was it. And too damn long without a woman. He must be, if he was susceptible to Rosie O'Hanlon. A woman in a foolish business who wore checkered socks and broken glasses. What the hell was the matter with him?

She came back and handed him a tall glass of water with ice and a twist of lemon. 'Are you all right?' She eyed him warily before going back to perch on the edge of the sofa.

'Fine. Sorry. I'm not usually so scattered.'

She stared at him a second, then stood as if she'd made a decision. 'I think you need to eat. I'm going to make us lunch,' she announced. 'You sit there and relax. It won't take me a minute.'

'No, thanks. I'd better go.' He started to get up. He didn't need lunch, or more time with this woman. He needed to leave. He only wished he'd been listening when she'd told him her idea about stopping the letters. Irritated with himself, he decided he'd call her later, say he wanted to go over it. She'd repeat what she'd told him and that would be that.

'Sit!' she ordered, peering at him through her ridiculous glasses. 'It's almost twelve-thirty. You have to eat. I have to eat. We'll eat together.'

Font groaned from the doorway and whomped his tail on the hardwood floor. 'Yes, and you too, Font,' she added.

'Look,' Kent protested. 'You don't have to do this.'

'I know.' She gave him a direct look and a sunny smile that hit his chest like a medicine ball. 'I want to. And I'm predicting if you don't eat now, you'll skip lunch entirely. Right?'

He nodded. 'It's been known to happen.'

'I'll bet.' She shook her head as if she disapproved, then headed toward the doorway she'd used to get the water. When she was through it, she popped her braced head back out. 'You're in luck, Summerton, my cooking is even better than my love letters.'

When she was gone, Kent sank back into the chair, his gaze on the empty doorway. A line from one of her letters jumped to mind. 'I'm hot, so fiercely hot! And I need you. Deep. In the moist place only you can know. Only you can have. Only you—'

Don't even think about it, Summerton. She's not your type. Not even close. He liked organization, ambition, focus. Unless he

28

guessed wrong, that didn't describe O'Hanlon. He hoisted his flattened resolve upright. He'd eat lunch and get out of here. That'd be the end of it.

A cold nose nuzzled his hand, then lifted his hand from the arm of the chair; the nose was Font's. Kent smiled and stroked the huge dog's bristly gray head. 'It's a good thing I didn't bring Lacy, big guy. She'd have been a goner.' *And one of us is enough for one day,* he added to himself.

Rosie was back, standing in the doorway, wiping her hands with a tea towel. 'Lunch is ready. Is eating at the kitchen table okay?'

'That'll be fine.' He pushed himself out of the chair and followed her into the kitchen. For the first time he took a good look around the house.

From the outside, the place had looked like an old, turn-of-the-century farmhouse, complete with peeling paint, gabled windows, and wide, uneven stairs leading to a wraparound porch. Inside, it was painted and papered into a cheerful home. Kent half expected to see a dozen kids stream in the front door and demand milk and cookies. But she had said Miss, meaning there was no Mister O'Hanlon kicking around. Okay, so he was glad. Didn't mean a damn thing. Font followed him into the big kitchen.

'Sit over there,' she instructed breezily, pointing to a chair at a round oak table in the

29

kitchen's alcove. He took the seat and Font collapsed at his feet. Kent reached down to rub under his ear and was rewarded with a groan that said, 'I'm yours for life.'

'I wouldn't want you to take that personally,' Rosie said, gesturing toward the dog. 'Old Font is a world-class con artist. He'll expect nothing less than half your lunch in exchange for letting you scratch his ear.' She ladled tomato soup into his bowl.

'Then I think he and Lacy would get along just fine.'

Rosie put a plate heaped with sandwiches in the middle of the table and sat down. She looked across at him and grinned before picking up her spoon and starting on her soup. 'So, you really do have a dog? An Irish wolfhound?' She shook her head, the neck brace automatically including her shoulders.

'That seems to amaze you. Why?'

She laughed softly, but looked at him carefully before she went on. 'I guess you look too neat, too organized, to have a mangy beast like that—' she gestured toward Font again '—clutter up your place.'

He tasted the soup. Delicious. Definitely not out of a can. 'And you're not?'

'Look around. Clutter is my life.'

He glanced around the kitchen. In one corner a half dozen shelves groaned under a load of cookbooks. The island in the center of the kitchen looked as though a team of chefs

30

was about to prepare a presidential banquet, and in the corner, by the big brick fireplace, a chair and carpet were buried under a library's supply of magazines and newspapers. She was right. His place was neater.

By the time his gaze got back to her, she was munching her sandwich and studying him. When he made no comment on her kitchen, she asked, 'Do you have one of those computerized schedulers? You know. Battery operated. The kind that beeps at you to remind you about appointments.' She lifted her hands in the air, putting a few inches of space between them. 'About this big,' she added.

'As a matter of fact, I do. Why?'

She slapped a hand on the table. 'I knew it!'

She was looking at him as if his pants were belted under his armpits and his hair was oiled. 'I take it there's something wrong with that?'

'Not wrong exactly. It's just what I expected.'

'Expected?'

'From talking to you on the phone. I figured you'd be a man of ambition and definite plans. The kind of man who knew exactly where he was going to be in five years.'

What she said was true, but he didn't admit it. After all, the lady hadn't made it sound like a compliment. 'You got all that from one phone call?'

'Uh-huh.' She took another bite of her sandwich and chewed quietly.

'And you don't approve?' He wished he could bite back the question. He didn't give a damn if she approved or not.

She put down her sandwich, put her elbows on the table, and laced her fingers together. Across this bridge, she gazed at him, her expression sober, introspective. 'It's not a question of approval. There's a part of me that envies you your ability to—' she glanced away briefly '—prioritize things. Get and keep control of life's messy threads. My accountant says that's exactly what I should be doing, but I'm not very good at it.'

'*You* have an accountant?'

'Does that surprise you?'

'About as much as my having a dog surprised you.'

She laughed at that, and it rang like a bell somewhere near his heart. Kent didn't know you could hear bells when you were sinking into quicksand. 'What else does your accountant think you should do?'

'For one thing, she thinks I should deep-six *Cyrano Inc.*'

'I'll second that.'

She ignored him. 'She also thinks I should sell this place. According to her, I'm mortgage poor.'

Kent looked around, this time more assessingly. 'Probably not a bad idea. It would bring top dollar in today's market.'

She was still smiling when she said, 'You and Jonesy would like each other.'

'Jonesy?'

'Roberta Jones. My accountant.' Her expression brightened. 'Maybe you'd like to meet her.'

Kent stared at her. 'Have I got this right? You met me less than an hour ago, and you're trying to fix me up with your accountant?'

'You'd like each other,' she repeated, her face earnest. 'Jonesy admires ambitious men with goals. She says that's the only kind of partner a smart woman should consider. She says in today's economy a blending of two careers makes more sense than a blending of hearts.'

He'd had enough. He was teed off. Here he was swimming upstream in a river of testosterone, and the cause of it was suggesting he go out with her accountant! 'I think I can arrange my own social life, Miss O'Hanlon.'

'Oops.' She wrinkled her nose and looked contrite. 'Sorry. Of course you can.' She stood. 'More soup?'

'No. Thanks.' He tossed his napkin on the table and rose to go. 'I think I'll leave before you call the marriage broker. I appreciate the lunch.'

She walked him to the door, Font ambling along behind them. Once there, she pushed her glasses up her nose and gazed up at him, her hand on the doorknob. The sunlight streamed through the side window, illuminating her sweater to neon.

'I didn't mean to embarrass you, or anything,' she said. 'I hope you know that.'

'You didn't.' One look through the mended glasses to her bright, somewhat worried blue eyes and his irritation dissolved. He couldn't help himself, he touched her cheek, drawing his index finger along her jawline. Her skin was dangerously soft. His touch seemed to disconcert her, but the neck brace made it awkward for her to pull away. He broke the connection reluctantly. 'Thanks for lunch, Rosie.'

She smiled then. 'I guess you can't be too mad if I'm Rosie again.'

'I guess not,' he said, and meant it.

He was opening his car door when he heard her call from the porch, 'What about the letters? You didn't tell me what you thought about my idea. Shall I do it or not?'

The letters. Damn! He didn't have a clue what her idea was. But then again . . .

He smiled and turned. 'I'll think about it and give you a call. Don't do anything until you hear from me. Okay?'

'Okay,' she yelled back.

*   *   *

Rosie watched him go, waving once as he left

34

her property and headed down the main road.

She stayed on the porch a long time, first standing, then easing herself into the big rocker near the door. Font flopped down beside her.

Her thoughts went here, there, and everywhere. It was as though she'd opened her door and a gale had blown through. Damn those eyes of his. She always was a sucker for green eyes.

'Too bad,' she said to Font, rubbing his ear. She leaned her head back. 'Yup, *really* too bad.'

Summerton wasn't her man, and that was unfortunate. Because if he were, it would put her ahead of schedule, and that would be terrific, because she wasn't getting any younger. She sighed. Why couldn't she have opened her door to the ideal man instead of an over-worked, over-tired corporate robot? She recognized the tension, the frayed edges. Summerton was programmed, hard-wired to a demanding job that barely left him time to eat. He had a computer scheduler, for heaven's sake. She swallowed her disappointment.

Jonesy would definitely have the hots for him. She pulled her lower lip under her teeth, wondering why she'd suggested they meet. A defensive gesture, she decided. After her last disastrous relationship with a set-the-world-on-fire type, she'd sworn off them for good. The mystery was that she always attracted

35

them. That they also attracted her, she chose to ignore.

Within weeks of being hired by MooreWrite, the VP of Sales had attached himself to her desk like moss to a ruin. So she'd decided to work at home. Lord, the man lived in a penthouse, wore Armani, and drove a Mercedes sedan—and he'd already gone through two wives. They were peanut butter and liverwurst.

And so were she and Kent Summerton, and that was a heartbreaker, because those eyes of his were to drown in, and that neural anesthetic he used for aftershave was—

Rosie yanked up her socks and pushed herself out of the rocker. It didn't matter what it was. He didn't make the cut. On that she would not compromise. It would probably shock the hell out of Jonesy, the prioritizer, and Summerton, the magnificent; but Rosie O'Hanlon had come up with a plan of her own.

And a man like Summerton, all edge and ambition, definitely wasn't part of it.

*   *   *

Kent phoned the following afternoon.

'I got another one of your letters today,' he said without preamble.

'They are *not* my letters. They are Gardenia's letters,' she stated flatly.

'I prefer to put a name with the prose,' he

36

said, his tone silky with a hint of tease.

Rosie rubbed one of her warming cheeks. For the first time, she realized this situation could get really embarrassing before it was over. Especially if he insisted on calling the letters hers. While romantic, the letters were also—at Gardenia's urging—rather bold. Some of her descriptions had made the top of Rosie's ears glow. She'd even told Rosie how big *it* was and just how she wanted *it* described. Of course, Rosie had swallowed her lies whole and jumped in with her usual excess of enthusiasm. How could she have been such a twit?

She pulled at her neck brace to let the steam escape so she could talk. 'Then use someone else's name,' she finally said. 'This one's taken.'

'Who's the lucky guy?'

'What? Oh, I meant taken by me.' *Damn it*, she should have lied. But she was no good at lying.

'Glad to hear it. Can I buy you dinner tonight? We'll discuss your idea. Make a decision.'

'No.'

'That's it? No?' He sounded stunned.

'The brace and I eat in.'

Silence.

'Then I'll come by tomorrow. We'll talk then.'

'I won't be here tomorrow. A colleague of

mine is coming to drive me to the office. It's our weekly project meeting.'

More silence. Rosie broke it. She shouldn't do this, but the sooner they could resolve the matter of Gardenia, the better. She hadn't liked the way her stomach lurched and fluttered when she'd picked up the phone and found him on the other end. No way was she going to be entered into that scheduler of his. A woman had to be strong.

'Why don't you come here for dinner?' she said, and found herself holding her breath.

'You're sure?'

'Yes.' *No*, she wasn't sure. This much lying she could handle. 'I haven't cooked for anyone since my surgery. It'll be fun.'

'Eight o'clock, okay? I've got a late meeting.'

Of course, you have, she thought. Men like you always have late meetings. And early ones. And weekend ones.

'Eight's fine,' she said. 'See you then.'

She clicked off the phone and looked at the clock. She had four hours, and, she told herself as she headed for her kitchen, creamed corn where her brain should be. She shouldn't have invited him here. What needed to be done about Gardenia could be done over the phone. She did *not* want to start something with Kent Summerton. And by inviting him to dinner, she had confirmed Jonesy's opinion of her. She *was* certifiable.

Font gave her a one-eyed stare from his sentry sleeping post in front of the fireplace. She registered it as disapproval. 'Be careful what you say, big guy. You're looking at the mess hall cook here.'

She opened the fridge door, which was enough incentive for him to rise on all fours and lumber over to help with the inventory.

'So what do you think?' She dug through the meat drawer. 'Lamb or beef?'

His tail whomped her thigh and he winked.

Rosie looked at the New York steaks in her hand, let out a long wistful breath, and nodded. 'You're right, Font, he's definitely a beefcake kind of guy.'

*   *   *

Later that night, when dinner was over, Kent had to agree with Rosie. She was a terrific cook. *And* she wrote great letters. When he'd gone back to the office yesterday afternoon, the first thing he'd done was reread every single one. Since meeting her, the letters had taken on a whole new meaning. Now he saw Rosie in every heated line. He'd almost be sorry to see the last of them. Almost.

After he'd helped with the dishes, she told him to go in the living room and relax while she had a few strong words with the brace. He was, she told him, driving her crazy. Kent ignored the fact she'd imbued the creation with human character—male at that—and did as she said, carrying in a tray bearing coffee and two pieces of what looked like the best peach pie he'd ever seen.

He sat on the sofa, barely resisting the urge to sprawl across it and close his eyes. He'd been up since five. If he didn't stay upright, he'd nod off for sure. He leaned forward, rested his elbows on his knees, and pressed his fingers against his closed eyes.

'You okay?' Rosie asked, walking into the room.

'A little tired but fine.' Tonight must be special, he thought wryly. She was wearing yellow and lime green socks. Striped. Real howlers. He suppressed a smile and watched her settle into the recliner and tuck her feet, atrocious socks and all, under her.

'Coffee?' he asked, nodding at the tray in front of him.

'I forgot.' She started to unwind from the chair.

'Stay where you are. I'll get it.' He poured for them both, then crossed the short distance separating them and gave her a steaming cup. Their fingers touched, and his gaze shifted to her face. When their eyes met, the air in his lungs heated uncomfortably. She looked away first.

'Thanks,' she said, pulling the coffee back from his hand and immediately raising the cup to her mouth. She didn't look at him again until he'd returned to the sofa.

'Want to talk about Gardenia now?' she asked.

He nodded and, ignoring his own coffee, leaned back to look at her, hands clasped behind his neck, legs stretched out in front of him. He could look at this lady for hours. Right now Gardenia was the last thing on his mind, but he'd put off the subject of the letters long enough.

He'd avoided it during dinner, deflecting the conversation from the merits of the Irish wolfhound to Rosie's opinion of Kent's eat-on-the-run diet, and how it was destroying his body. They'd talked about Rosie's mother. Quite a woman, by Rosie's account. After Rosie's father's death, she'd worked night and day to convert an old, rundown hotel into one of the best in Seattle. Rosie was obviously proud of what she'd done, although there were hints of a pretty lonely Rosie as a kid. He'd like to know more about that, but for now Gardenia was up. He cursed silently and rubbed his jaw.

Once they settled the Gardenia thing, he probably would never see this woman again. And something in him didn't want that to happen.

His gut clenched, and he dropped his head. He'd have to ask her out. Hell, even the idea of dating wearied him, the doing of it would put him under. Women. Dating. They took

41

time, and he just plain didn't have any right now. He stifled a yawn.

'So, now that you've thought about it, what do you think? Do you agree with my plan, or not?' She sipped her coffee and stared at him over the rim of the cup.

'I might. If I had any idea what it was.'

She looked confused, and two fine vertical lines met in her forehead. 'But I told you all about it yesterday.'

'I was distracted—' he looked in the general direction of her feet '—by your socks.' He slumped deeper into the sofa.

She stuck out a foot and rotated it as if to study her bilious green and yellow footwear. 'Can't see why. Look pretty ordinary to me.'

Kent eyed her from under heavy eyelids. 'Rosie, there's nothing ordinary about you.' God, he was sleepy.

She pulled her foot back. 'The letters, Kent. Let's talk about the letters.'

He nodded. 'Right. So tell me this good idea of yours.'

'What I think we should do is . . .

*   *   *

Kent woke up to sunlight doing laser surgery on his irises. He shaded his eyes against the glare coming at him from the living room window, pulled himself to a sitting position, and looked around stupidly. He was on Rosie's

42

couch. He rubbed his eyes, then fingercombed his hair.

Smooth, Summerton, real smooth.

A glance at his watch told him it was after seven. He should have been at Beachline an hour ago. The smell of coffee and frying bacon lured his nose—followed closely by the rest of him—to the kitchen while he tucked his shirt back into his pants.

Rosie was at the stove, pulling something from the oven with hands engulfed in a pair of the biggest oven mitts he'd ever seen. Out came plump muffins and an aroma that was all about lazy Sunday mornings, scattered newspapers, and crumbs in the bed. Kent, leaning against the doorjamb, breathed deep.

Rosie caught sight of him as she turned to put the muffins on the counter. 'Hey, it's the dinner guest from hell.' She waved a mitted hand. 'There's orange juice in the fridge.'

'Fresh squeezed, I'll bet.'

She smiled at him. 'You're complaining?' She used one of her mittened paws to push back a rush of red hair that threatened to cloud her face.

'Mind if I use your shower first? Mess up some towels. Maybe splash some water around?'

'Do your worst. You'll find what you need down the hall off the guest bedroom.'

The shower made him feel human. An idiot human, maybe, but it was an improvement.

Back in the kitchen, he ambled to the fridge in stockinged feet and poured himself the juice she'd offered. He leaned against the fridge, sipping and enjoying the sight of Rosie O'Hanlon in the morning. Nice. Very nice.

'I owe you an apology,' he said.

She smiled at that, and her expression turned impish. 'For what? Sleeping on my sofa or nodding off before I finished my first complete sentence. That *was* a first. Most men hang in there for at least a paragraph or two.'

He grimaced at her teasing words, then drained the last of his orange juice. 'Both.'

'That's okay. Sit down, hotshot.'

He watched her take a warmed plate from the oven, fill it with eggs, bacon, and fried tomato, then put it on a place mat at the same seat he'd used last night.

She gave him a stern look. 'Eat—and then run.' She took off the mitts and hung them on a hook by the stove. 'I've got to get myself dressed for the corporate jungle. My ride's due in about a half an hour.' She turned to face him. 'If you need anything else, you're on your own. Okay?'

'Okay.' He gestured toward the table. 'This is nice, Rosie. You didn't have—'

'—to do it. I know.'

Their gazes met and locked. Kent saw a faint blush color her cheeks. She looked pensive, as if unsure of her next move—or his. Kent wasn't.

He wanted the food, but he wanted something else a hell of a lot more. Something equally as basic. He walked toward her. He needed to touch her. To taste her. Right here. Now.

She stood, a flame-haired statue, still and waiting. At least he hoped she was.

'Rosie?' He touched her cheek with his knuckles, closed his eyes to imprint the softness of skin to memory. He heard her intake of breath. 'Rosie,' he said again, brushing his mouth over hers.

He wanted to slide his hand to the back of her neck, pull her close, but the brace was a barrier, so he took her face in his palms and slipped his fingers into her hair at her temples. Tendrils wrapped around his fingers like breeze-blown smoke.

He pulled back and looked down at her. 'I have to kiss you. You know that.' His voice came from a closed throat and sounded strangely uneven.

She gulped and tightened her lips, but she didn't move back. Not an inch. Thank God. Then she gave the barest of nods, her chin pressing into the brace. Her expression was wary—as if she were about to receive her first dose of an unknown medicine. Her hands fisted at her sides.

He smiled, sensing she hoped it would taste bad. That *he* would taste bad.

And he kissed her, determined to prove her

wrong.

He took her mouth gently, willing her lips to ease and welcome his. He tamped his impatience, the knot of need forming in his gut. He slipped his fingers deeper into her hair, anchoring her head to better explore and savor. His eyes closed, shutting out the cheery kitchen, the breakfast on the table. Shutting out everything but Rosie and the sweetness of her mouth. His breathing thickened, and the knot pulled painfully. He felt her stiffen and pull back, and a stab of disappointment jolted him.

He was steeling himself to release her when he heard a low moan, and felt her breath rush across his cheek.

'Oh, Kent, this is—' She didn't finish. Instead, she wrapped her arms tight around him, pressed her body to his, and parted her lips.

His body hardened to aching, and he groaned into her mouth, pulling her closer. She came, rested flush against him until he could feel the heat of her. His tongue tested the warmth in her mouth, silk and moist. Then her hands moved over his buttocks.

His grip tightened—everything tightened— and he shifted his mouth over hers and tugged and nibbled at her lower lip, probed deeper, then deeper yet. He wanted more.

'Ouch!'

The word didn't fit. It took a second for it to

46

register.

Her neck. Damn it, he'd hurt her!

He released her abruptly, but held her upper arms while he tried to even out his breathing. She eased back slowly, grimacing.

'I hurt you.' He cursed. He was an idiot. Godzilla in heat. What in hell made men so damn clumsy, anyway? But he knew, in this case, it was Rosie. If he'd hurt her, he swore he'd never try anything like this again—until he had a permission slip from her doctor.

'No,' she said, but her hand flew to the back of the brace and her face was all scrunched and rigid.

'Damn it, Red, I did hurt you. Get your coat. I'm taking you to your doctor.'

'I'm fine,' she repeated, her voice stronger now. 'Just snarled up. Lend me a hand, would you? And get my hair out from under this conning tower I've got around my neck.' She turned her back on him and lifted her hair from her nape.

As he carefully untangled her hair, he said, 'You're *absolutely* certain I didn't hurt you?'

'Positive. You'd need wire cutters and a blow torch to get to me through this.' She faced him then, her hair frazzled, her face delectably pink.

'Thank God.' He touched her cheek, but she stepped away, her expression wary again.

'I knew you were trouble, you know. The minute I caught that scent you wear.'

47

'I don't wear scent.' He reached for her again, and she put a chair between them. 'We shouldn't have started something neither of us can finish,' she said, lifting her gaze to his, her expression stern as a preacher's.

He grinned. 'Not true. I'm a great finisher.'

'Then take up woodworking.' She stepped briskly from behind the chair and headed for the door. 'I'm going to get ready for work.' She wobbled and bumped a shoulder against the doorjamb, but she didn't look back.

Kent watched her disappear through the kitchen doorway, disappointed she wasn't going to eat with him, but not surprised. Probably just as well, because he needed to cool down. And unless he was miles off base, so did she. He tucked into the breakfast she'd left him. Thank God he hadn't hurt her, because it would have been hell to keep that promise. He liked Rosie O'Hanlon. He liked her a lot.

It occurred to him that in less than forty-eight hours he'd eaten here three times. That put him dangerously close to freeloader status. Strange, too, that he was more rested after sleeping on Rosie's couch than he was after a night in his king-sized bed.

He looked at his watch. Over an hour late. He picked up his pace. Marlene probably had an APB out on him by now.

He was putting his dishes in the dishwasher when Rosie rushed back to the kitchen. If his kiss had made an impression, she gave no sign of it—other than to keep a good ten feet between them.

'Hennessy's outside,' she announced. 'Gotta go. Can you see yourself out? Do I look okay? There are no labels sticking out or anything is there?'

Gone were the outrageous socks and green pants. In their place were a long, loose skirt and an oversized white shirt tied at the waist. She'd pulled her hair into a topknot resembling a badly engineered waterfall and used a blue scarf to camouflage part of her neck brace. He lowered his gaze. And she was wearing shoes, sneakers with scorching yellow laces—and red toe caps. He shook his head.

'You look great. Corporate America will never be the same.'

'Thanks. You *can* see yourself out, can't you?'

He nodded, and she rushed for the door.

'Oh, I almost forgot.' She turned back. 'Would you write down your fax number and leave it on the kitchen table?'

'My fax number?'

'I'm going to fax you my idea about Gardenia's letters. Then, between naps and other distractions, you can read it and let me know what you think by return fax. Good idea?'

Kent thought it was a lousy idea, but neither he nor she had time to argue.

CHAPTER FOUR

Her fax came at five o'clock that afternoon.

Kent:
Here's the plan. I still have Gardenia's post
office box number. While there is no
guarantee she's still using it, I suggest I send
a letter there, telling her you've traced her
to *Cyrano* and want the letters to stop
immediately. I'll offer to return her money
if she complies—and promise not to tear
her hair out for lying to me (about you
being her fiancé) in the first place. (That
last bit is personal!) So, what do you think?
My fax awaits your fax.

Rosie O'Hanlon

Kent quickly scribbled a reply.

Rosie:
Sounds good. Go for it. I'll let you know if it
works. In the meantime, I owe you three—
count 'em—three meals. If Brace can go to
business meetings, surely he can go out to
dinner. Vin Santo's at seven sound okay?

Kent

P.S. I got another letter today. This makes
number twelve and the second one this
week. Gardenia, it seems, has decided to

turn up the heat. You *do* have a way with words, O'Hanlon. I liked the bit about 'lying naked in a storm of moonlight and music.' Can I ask if this is something you've personally experienced?

Rosie faxed back immediately. There was no reference to the content of her letters—or Kent's question.

Kent:
Brace and I thank you for the invitation, but Vin Santo's is out. I'll write Gardenia today. Let me know if the letters stop. If they don't, I'll go to plan B (if I can come up with one!) and fax it to you.

Rosie.

Kent read the terse fax, then tossed it onto his organized desk and glared at it. So she wouldn't have dinner with him. Probably just as well. Rosie O'Hanlon wasn't his type anyway—all bright color and chaos. He could live without it.

Without her.

He walked to the window of his office, propped a shoulder against the frame, and looked out over the emerald green of the golf course. The dinner invitation was a courtesy. Nothing more. No need to see her again. Screw the eye contact—a modem would do. Much more efficient. He should be grateful

51

O'Hanlon felt the same way. He scowled. So, why wasn't he? What he felt was rejected. And damn it, it hurt.

He heard a rap on his opened door.

'Kent, you busy?' Marlene asked. 'Or are you still looking for Con?' She used her head to gesture toward the golf course view he'd been staring at, but not seeing, for the last few minutes. 'If you are, you should know he just left for Hawaii.'

'Hawaii? What's he doing in Hawaii?'

'I haven't a clue.'

There was the usual stab of frustration at Con's growing lack of responsibility, but this time no anger. Just weary acceptance. He'd managed the workload so far. He'd just carry on. What tattered remains of a personal life he'd once enjoyed had long since disintegrated. In that department he had nothing more to lose.

A surge of regret swept through him, leaving in its wake a kaleidoscope image of red hair and a chorus line of wide smiles wearing Technicolor socks. Rosie was in there somewhere.

'Oh, and your mother called.' Marlene glanced at the message in her hand. 'She said to remind you it's your turn and to call if you need her help for anything.'

The family barbecue. He'd almost forgotten. Of course there wasn't a chance in hell his mother would. It was a yearly event,

52

and you missed it on risk of excommunication as he'd discovered last year. He'd had to leave on a business trip—and he was *still* hearing about it. No way out this year, because it was his year to host. Just what he needed. An AWOL partner, a madcap woman who'd managed to etch herself into his mind—and the damn barbecue.

'There's more.' Marlene said.

'I'm sure there is.' Kent sat in his chair and motioned Marlene to the one beside his desk.

'You remember that computerized tee-off system I told you about? The one for the pro shop? Con bought it.'

Kent took a calming breath. 'And?'

'And it's incomprehensible. From the write-up and initial spec sheets, the system actually looks okay. But as you know, I wasn't too keen about it in the first place and now I know why.'

'So, what's the problem?'

'The documentation. It might as well be written in ancient Aramaic. And because the program's intended to book tee times from the pro shop, the hotel's front desk—and interactively from the rooms—the *how-to* aspect is critical. Without it we'll have a total screw up on our hands.' She paused. 'And hell hath no fury like a golfer without his appointed tee time.'

Kent's spine wasn't the only thing straightening as Marlene continued to speak. So were his thoughts. For the first time in a long while, Con York had done something right. Kent tilted back in his swivel chair, looked at the ceiling, and smiled.

'You're taking this well,' Marlene said. 'I'd have thought you'd be walking on the ceiling rather than smiling at it.'

'It happens I have a solution to this problem.' He stood. 'Leave it to me.'

She gave him a questioning glance, shrugged, and stood, then put a sheaf of papers on his desk. 'Given that you're in a problem-solving mood, take a look at these. The new wing is now officially over budget and behind schedule. Packard wants to see you tomorrow. To explain things, he says.' Packard was the contractor.

Kent picked up the papers. His gut tensed. Packard was a problem he didn't need. Damn shifty-eyed—

'What shall I tell him?' Marlene asked.

'Tell him I can't wait to hear his latest excuse,' he said wryly. He pushed a couple of keys on his scheduler. 'Tell him six-thirty tomorrow morning.'

'Will do.' She hesitated at the door. 'I'm having an early dinner in the dining room. Join me?'

'Not tonight. Thanks. I'll have Mae bring something to my office.' He lifted the sheaf of papers she'd given him and dropped them again. 'Looks like I'll be here awhile.' Midnight, at least, he figured. By morning he'd

54

have memorized every number in the file.

'See you tomorrow then.'

When she'd left, Kent shoved the papers aside. For the moment, his priority was finding the telephone number for MooreWrite Technical Writers, Inc.

*   *   *

Rosie sealed the letter to Gardenia and put it with the one to her mother, one she'd finally finished writing after a week of stops and starts. Of course, she could just phone her, and often did, but she knew her mother enjoyed receiving her breezy letters as much as she enjoyed writing them. She always mailed them to the hotel, and Rosie could see her mother's smile when this one arrived on her desk. The envelope was a fluorescent sunrise yellow with a polka dot rainbow. Just the thing to brighten a busy executive's day. Rosie knew it would be the first piece of mail she'd open. In contrast, Gardenia's letter was in a plain white number ten. Very businesslike. She hoped, for Kent's sake, her plan would work.

She gave the letters a final straightening and went to the window. The day was light gray, the sun a pale glow behind the curtain of cloud. Rosie was certain the sun would take center stage by noon. Her gaze fixed on the dimly lit cloud.

You should have gone to dinner with him.

The thought bounced into her head and thudded to a hard stop. She couldn't budge it. While her Lady Brain, rational as always, told her Kent Summerton was a suit and most definitely not the man of her dreams—or her plans—Hormone, the unconscionable tart, put up an argument from below. What suit? she asked. The man didn't even wear a suit. Maybe he didn't wear it on the outside, Lady Brain said knowingly, but inside? A three-piecer, including club tie and wing tips.

Mom would love him. She could see them now, discussing the economy, management theories, return on investment, marketing strategies and—God forbid—the current price of real estate. She shuddered and shoved the ugly image aside. Brain was absolutely right. Going to dinner with Kent would be a waste of her time. And at twenty-eight, considering her agenda, she couldn't afford to waste a minute on the wrong guy.

'Thank you, Lady Brain,' she said aloud, then headed to the door to let Font in before settling down to work. Nothing like a blinking cursor to nail down a wandering mind.

*   *   *

The next morning at breakfast her phone rang.
'Rosie, it's me.' The me was Hennessy.
'Hey. What's happening?' She shoved aside the crossword she was working on and sipped

some coffee.

'At the meeting you said you'd take on an extra project, if one came along.'

'I did. I live for my work, Hennessy.'

'Don't we all,' he said. 'Anyway, I've got one for you. Actually, the guy requested you specifically.'

Rosie picked up a pen and idly tapped it on the newspaper. 'Nice to be recognized,' she said. 'Who is it?'

'Beachline Resort. That posh place where I took you to lunch when you first signed on with us? Remember?'

Rosie dropped the pen and leaned back in her chair. 'I remember. Let me guess. The guy who called was Kent Summerton, right?'

'Right. How'd you know that?'

Okay, so she was pleased. A gut female reaction. Nothing more. 'Never mind. But satisfy my curiosity, Hennessy. What on earth would a resort like that need a tech writer for?' Be interesting to see just how inventive the man was.

'The usual. They bought a computer application with lousy documentation, and they want it rewritten so their people can work with it. Interested?'

'*Not.* Tell Mr. Summerton he'll have to get someone else. I've got a full schedule as it is.' Thank you again, Lady Brain, Rosie said silently. Nice to know you're there when I need you.

57

'Am I missing something here? Did you, or did you not, want extra work?'

'I did. But a piece of that government stuff will do fine.'

'No can do.'

'What? Why?'

'Assigned. Besides, they cut back the contract by about forty percent.'

'Damn!'

'That's what I said. So back to this Beachline thing. You want it?'

'No.'

'They'll pay a premium. Said they want it done pronto.'

A vision of her bank statement danced in her head. She sighed. 'Okay, okay. I'm had.'

'Want the telephone number?'

'No. I've got it. Thanks, Hennessy.'

'Thank *you*, Rosie girl. The company can use the revenue. See ya.'

Rosie clicked off then clicked on. She ignored it, but something a lot like anticipation wriggled in her chest.

'Mr. Summerton, please.'

She expected another melody from the Blue Danube, but Kent came on the line immediately.

'Summerton,' he said, sounding busy and preoccupied. Rosie sighed again, curled her fingers tighter over the phone. Even his voice affected her. *Something* was making her elbows sweat. Well, sweat or no sweat, she told herself

58

firmly she would do this job and not make a damn fool out of herself while she was at it.

'Hello, I—'

'—Rosie?'

'Brace and all. Seems like you just hired yourself a technical writer, Summerton.'

'And from what that Hennessy guy said, a damned good one. When can we meet?'

She *heard* him smile. She swore she did. 'You'll have to come here.'

'I'm getting used to that.'

'Yes, well, don't get *too* used to it. This is a project, a *business* project, nothing more.'

'Of course. Did I say anything to make you think otherwise?' he asked, his tone cool and satiny.

'No, I guess not,' she said, wishing he was less smooth and she more sharp.

Then again, she was no doubt reading more into this than she should. All he'd really done was ask her out for dinner—a simple courtesy. There was the KISS, of course. But one searing kiss did not a relationship make. Besides, guys were preprogrammed to kiss any female within reach who fell short of gargoyle status. And they'd been known to drop the gargoyle standard in a pinch. He wanted to hire her. Not unusual. She was a technical writer, after all. What could be more natural?

But her instincts were sniffing the breeze. Okay, so she was up to her sock tops in attraction to this man. It didn't mean a thing.

He'd run a mile if he knew what was on her agenda.

Maybe you should tell him.

Lady Brain was a real pain in the butt at times. But in this instance, she was right. It was time to tell Summerton her plan and exactly how he *did not* fit into it. But to do it, she needed to see the green of his eyes.

At least that's what Lady Brain said. Or was it that other, less reliable part of her anatomy?

'Then if you're satisfied I have no ulterior motive,' he went on. 'When shall I drop off this heap of manual I have sitting on my desk.'

'You can come by tonight about seven-thirty—if that's okay with your scheduler.'

'It's okay. See you then.' A pause. 'I'm looking forward to working with you, Rosie. And believe it or not, I really do need your expertise on this.'

'You'll get it.'

'Good.' He paused, seeming reluctant to break off. 'See you tonight, then.' His tone would have fluffed silk.

'Tonight,' Rosie confirmed, wishing he didn't have a voice that curled through the line and cut off her breathing, wishing her own voice didn't have whispers at its edge.

Neither said good-bye. Both disconnected.

Rosie glared down at Font, who had come in to warm her toes.

'I will not primp or preen. Do you hear me? And I will not have butterflies in my tummy like a star-struck groupie. *And* I will *not* make dinner for the man,' she vowed, poking him with her foot. 'This is absolutely, positively not a date. Is that clear?'

Font opened one bleary eye and winked it before closing it again.

*   *   *

She made salad and roast beef steeped in garlic, surrounded it with perfect new potatoes.

She baked a cheesecake.

She vacuumed.

She fussed with her hair.

She peeled her face.

She hated herself.

Kent arrived ten minutes early with a hundred-pound manual and a bottle of fine French wine.

She glared at him, leaving him to stand in the doorway. 'What's that for?' she asked, looking at the wine bottle as if it were a vibrator and she a nun.

He studied her a moment. 'Target practice?' he said, something close to a smile lurking about his mouth.

'That's good, Summerton. That's very good.' She let out a breath. She was being a jerk and knew it. There was definitely no cause to be rude. Wine was a perfectly acceptable thing to bring to dinner. But then again, who'd said anything about dinner?

Still standing in the doorway, he lifted his nose and sniffed appreciatively. 'Smells good. Expecting anyone special?' His gaze was steady.

'Just trying to save a life.'

His expression turned quizzical.

'Yours, Summerton. Now that you're a paying customer, it's in my interest to keep you healthy.'

He looked into her eyes and smiled. 'I'm healthy, Rosie, very healthy.' The fullness of his smile, its intimacy, made her breath gather in her throat. With no oxygen reaching Lady Brain, she made a quick exit. As for Hormone, the trollop, that smile had her putting on lipstick and a black teddy.

Rosie O'Hanlon finally admitted she was on a slippery slope with no handrails. Kent Summerton might not be the man of her plans, but he came frighteningly close to being the man of her dreams.

'So, do I come in or are you giving me take-out?'

She realized then, that he was still standing in the open doorway. She waved him in, took the manual from him, and directed him to the living room. 'Make yourself comfortable.' She gave him a stern look. 'But not too comfortable. No sleeping until you're safe in your own bed.'

He raised his right hand, nodded solemnly.

62

'Sit down, I'll just be a minute.'

She closed the front door after him and turned to watch as he took a seat on the sofa, resting an ankle on his opposite knee in that peculiarly male way. There was a rightness to him being in her house, sitting on her sofa that baffled her. He wasn't right at all.

When he looked up and caught her watching him, she hustled herself into the kitchen. Once there, Lady Brain took over, reminding her of her plan to lay some straight talk on Mr. Button-Down. After that, she expected the last she'd see of Kent Summerton would be the blur of tail lights and a blast of exhaust fumes.

But it could wait until after dinner.

*　　*　　*

'Did you get a letter today?' Rosie asked. They'd finished eating and were back in the living room. She in the recliner, Kent back on the sofa. Both were sipping wine. They'd discussed the documentation project through dinner. That topic exhausted, Gardenia was obviously next up.

'Not today. But I'm due for one. Our Gardenia is reliable to a fault. Did you mail your letter?'

'Last night. If she gets it—and if she pays any attention to it—the letters should stop by the end of next week.' She ran her index finger inside and along the top of the brace where it chafed her neck.

'Uncomfortable?' Kent asked.

'A nuisance more than anything. I can't wait to get rid of the darn thing. There are times I think an out-of-whack disc would be easier to deal with.'

'I doubt it.' He shifted and leaned his head against the sofa back, studying her through narrowed lids. 'When it comes off, are you going to be a hundred percent?'

'So the doctor man says.'

'I'm glad.'

The way he said 'I'm glad' made it sound as if he had a vested interest in her recovery. She reminded herself he didn't. 'Let's talk about Gardenia. She's much more interesting than my back.'

He lifted a dark brow and grinned. 'Oh, I don't know. I think your back is fascinating.'

Okay, that was definitely seductive. She eyed him, knowing she looked leery and suspicious. 'What exactly do you want from me, Summerton?'

'Want?' He drank some wine.

'Do you want to go to bed with me? Is that it?'

He didn't move a muscle, just continued to gaze at her from under those enviable long lashes of his. 'You really cut to the chase, don't you?'

'I'm not going to, you know,' she stated

firmly. 'You should know that up front. I'll help you with the Gardenia business. I'll do the project for Beachline, but the bed bit is definitely out.'

'Why?'

'Why?' she repeated, taken aback by his calm question.

'That's what I said.'

'How about because I don't want to?'

He appeared to consider that. 'I don't think so.'

'No one can say you lack in the self-esteem department.'

'No. They can't.' He waited, his gaze unnervingly direct. 'So, why won't you go to bed with me?'

Okay, she thought, here goes. 'Because the next man I sleep with will be either my husband or my husband-to-be.

'I see. No more test flights, is that it?'

'You got it.'

'Too bad. I'm a hell of a pilot,' he grinned.

Rosie stifled a grin. That was her problem. She was always too lighthearted, too willing to laugh. But not about this new plan of hers. She had an agenda, and she intended to stick to it.

'There's more to life than flying,' she said, determinedly sober.

'Like what?'

'Kids. Lots of kids.' She waved a hand to gesture around the big old house. 'I want to fill this place with children, and I want a husband

65

who wants that, too.'

'Kids,' he repeated vacantly, as if the concept of procreation was entirely new.

'No, not just kids. *Lots and lots of kids.*' She was on a roll.

'Define "lots."'

'Ten. Preferably a dozen,' she said, using the double digits for effect. It worked.

Rosie swore he turned pale. Her heart twisted painfully. She had, to admit she was disappointed. Some addled part of her had hoped he'd say, great, let's get started. Instead, he looked dazed.

'That's not a family, O'Hanlon, that's a regiment—and perpetual pregnancy. You're kidding, right?'

'Wrong. I want those kids, every single one of them.'

He took a deep breath and shook his head. 'I don't believe it.' She had the feeling he was talking to himself.

She soldiered on. 'The point *is* I intend to be a full-time wife and mother. And I want a man who *wants me* to be that and is willing to support it with his heart, his head, his time, and his wallet.'

'Don't forget sperm count.'

She lifted her chin. 'That, too.'

He almost smiled, then turned serious. 'So, you don't want to work after you get married?'

'You don't think raising kids—especially today—is work?'

'You know what I mean. Most women today want a satisfying professional life.'

'Exactly. And what I want is to raise my kids with all the dedication and professionalism I can muster. Name one thing more satisfying than that.'

'Kids are expensive. Today's economics—'

'Hah! I knew it. Money. Trust someone who doesn't like kids to talk about how much they cost.'

'Did I say I didn't like kids?'

'You didn't have to.'

He let out a long breath. 'I was just trying to make the point that there's a monetary component to every decision we make, like it or not.'

She snorted in a most inelegant way. Her world was already crammed with people who reduced everything to economics. She didn't need another one.

He leaned forward, his look speculative. 'Tell me something, O'Hanlon, is there a practical bone in your body?'

She grinned, giving him a proud look. 'Not one.'

He frowned as if her answer was exactly what he expected, then asked, 'Why are you telling me this?'

'I'd think it was obvious.'

He smiled thinly and nodded. 'You've decided my sperm count isn't up to the job?'

'I'm sure your, uh, count is perfectly

adequate for—let me guess—one child. Later, of course, when it's convenient and there's enough saved for the lonely little soul's college fund?'

Her heart held its place while she waited for his denial. It didn't come.

'Any idea where you're going to find this supportive father figure?' he finally asked.

'Not a clue. But I know he's out there. And as soon as this—' she tapped her neck brace '—is off, I'm setting out to find him.'

He gave her a speculative look. 'How much longer do you have to wear the brace?'

'Less than three weeks.'

Kent's frown deepened to a scowl. Rosie had no idea what he was thinking.

CHAPTER FIVE

Monday morning, Rosie woke up with the cold of the century. She was convinced that sometime during the night she'd had a brain transplant, and the new one didn't fit. She sneezed, blew, and coughed her way to the bathroom. She wouldn't feel so bad had she managed to get some sleep. But sleep was in short supply ever since Kent left her house last Friday. He'd nearly sucked her and Font up his exhaust in his haste to get out of her driveway. The irritating part was he hadn't left her

68

thoughts. Hormone, the sleazy harlot, woke her at all hours. Summerton might as well have played pilot after all. At least then she'd have a concrete reason to feel like an overused sponge.

In the kitchen she downed a tall glass of orange juice, then, between nose blowings, made herself tea and toasted a crumpet she couldn't eat. She sat at the table and tried to make sense of the morning crossword. No go. She shoved it aside and carried her mug of tea into her office. The Beachline manual stared at her from beside her computer. Darn thing was the size of a New York phone book. She sighed. It was after nine o'clock, and Jonesy was due at ten. She should get started.

Font ambled in and leaned into her side.

Together they blearily eyed the lump of manual. 'We're gobing for a balk, Font. A log balk.'

Font gave her a you-don't-have-to-ask-me-twice look and switched to puppy mode, everything twitching at once. With a better than hundred-pound dog, this wasn't cute. Rosie picked up her pace, and in seconds they were on the porch, just in time to see Kent's Saab pull up to the lower step.

Just what she needed—a heart rush to go with her head cold.

What was he doing here? He'd hardly said a word after her announcement about the family she planned to have someday. He'd turned

69

quite surly in fact. She'd figured from there on their relationship would go completely electronic. But here he was, opening his car door in her driveway.

She watched him through a gray mist, stirred by an undeniable longing. Why couldn't he have been the one? But he wasn't. She knew that the moment he free-associated the word 'kids' with a cost benefit analysis.

Why couldn't he have looked out and imagined the pastures around her house filled with happy children, safe and loved? Why couldn't he have wanted what she wanted?

She blew her nose. Well, it didn't matter. Things were as they were, and she wasn't about to try and convince Kent Summerton, or any other man, they should have a pack of kids. Her future husband, whoever he might be, had to want them as much as she did. Otherwise, it would be a recipe for disaster.

Kent got out of his car and made a dash for the front porch. He shook the rain from his dark hair and a drop of it hit Rosie's cheek. He looked surprised to see her there.

'What are you doing here?' he asked.

'I lib here,' she said, poking at her nose with a tissue. One thing about having a cold: she couldn't smell his delicious aftershave. Every defense helped.

'I know that, Rosie,' he said with an irritating lift of his eyebrows. 'I mean what are you doing outside—' he waved a hand '—in

70

this. Where are you going?'

Until now, Rosie hadn't noticed it was raining, really raining. She lifted her chin. 'Bor a balk. Wanta gum?'

'Excuse me?'

Rosie sneezed and nearly blew what was left of her brains out. The top of her head definitely loosened.

Kent took her arm. 'I'm going to enroll you in Nutcases Anonymous if you don't get your buns in there—fast.' He opened the front door and steered her inside, his hand firmly in the small of her back. Font's tail dropped earthward. He gave them a baleful look before following them inside.

'Sorry, big guy, but the lady comes first.'

Rosie sneezed again, but she took her jacket off. He was right. It was a deluge out there, and she couldn't afford to die of pneumonia. Jonesy would kill her.

'I'm going to make you a hot drink, and you're going to take it easy. Got that?'

'You're gonna bhat?'

'Make you a hot drink.'

'Dobn't that neeb a stobe?'

'You have a stove, and for your information I know how to heat an element.'

'Burrumph.' Rosie blew her nose. Kent looked skyward.

'I take that—whatever it was—as an insult. But I *can* boil water, and that's what I'm about to do. Hot water, lemon, and honey.' He

71

steered Rosie to the kitchen. 'And some time in bed. According to my mother, it never fails.'

'Sounds goob.' Rosie was thinking her mother would have bought her a box of tissues and headed to the office. Running a business and having to support a daughter on her own had never left her with any alternative.

The suggestion of time in bed sounded good, too, rolling as it did from a pair of lips that tasted like spearmint and midnight promises.

Kent commandeered her kitchen while Rosie watched dully. He was surprisingly efficient, and in minutes she was downing the Summerton cure for the common cold. Not exactly ambrosia, but soothing.

'What are you dobing here, anyway?' she finally asked.

'You sound better already,' he said, looking smug. 'Good thing I came along in time to save your miserable life.' He took a drink of the coffee he'd made while Rosie sat watching him like a Monday drunk. 'When did you go into self-destruct mode, anyway?'

'I neebed some fresh air.'

Kent looked at the window where rain coursed over the glass as if someone had turned a hose on it. 'Fresh, huh? Normal people would notice that it's a bit damp out there.'

'I dibn't look before I leabed.' She blew again.

'Now why doesn't that surprise me? Drink up, O'Hanlon. Then go back to bed for an hour or so.'

Rosie sniffed and stood. 'Okay. But you dibn't answer me. What are you dobing here?'

He hesitated. 'I can't find my scheduler. I thought maybe I'd left it here.'

Rosie shook her head. 'Nob here. Guess you'll hab to geb along widout it, Hobshot.'

His lips twitched. 'Guess so. Now hit the sack, Red. If you don't mind, I'd like to make a couple of calls before I go.'

'Be my best.' Rosie headed for the bedroom. He'd called her Red, but then every man who ever spent more than ten minutes in the company of her hair usually did. Normally, she hated it. His using it should have irritated her. It didn't. Get a grip, Rosaleen, the man drove all the way out here in a monsoon looking for his stupid scheduler. There was no hope for him.

*　　　*　　　*

About an hour later, when Rosie got up—much improved—Kent was still there. So was Jonesy. They were sitting at her kitchen table, looking at each other as if they'd discovered a new candy—and were just now finalizing the distribution system. Rosie's heart slipped silently into her socks. She knew they'd like each other. Economically speaking, they were a perfect pairing. Like the Dow Jones and Warren Buffet.

'Better?' Kent asked, getting up when she stepped into the room.

Rosie breathed deeply. Her sinuses had unclogged at last, and her voice was back to normal.

'Much. Thanks. I added a cold tablet to your mom's cure-all. I'm almost human.' She tugged at the brace. 'Or should I say humanoid.'

'Won't be long before it's off, Rosaleen,' Jonesy said, sipping her coffee and looking back and forth between her and Kent.

'No, not long.' Rosie didn't sit. Instead, she ran a finger along the edge of the table. 'I take it introductions aren't necessary.'

They nodded and smiled at each other. 'Now you've got company, I'll head back to work.' He walked over to Rosie, took her by the shoulders, and kissed her cheek, whispering, 'Take care of yourself.'

She swallowed, scarcely able to breathe. Her cheek was hot where his mouth had lingered. 'I will.' Was that thin, reedy voice truly hers? She cleared her throat.

'When do you expect to have the manual complete?' He shrugged into his jacket and headed for the door.

'I don't know yet. I need to have a good look at it. I'll let you know.'

He nodded, and for a moment it looked as

though he were going to say something, then he smiled at Jonesy who'd come up behind them. 'Nice meeting you, Jonesy.'

With that, he was gone.

When the door closed behind him, Rosie went to the window, pushed the curtain aside, and watched him sprint through the rain to his car. He moved well, she thought, quick and fluid. Kent Summerton was a man in a hurry.

'Earth to Rosie. Earth to Rosie.'

Rosie settled her gaze on Jonesy and blinked. 'Sorry. Wool-gathering. What did you say?'

'I said who is that?'

Rosie headed for the kitchen and Jonesy followed her like a goose in formation. 'I though you introduced yourselves.'

'We did. I know his name, what he does, but that's it. I need more, Rosie. Much, much more.'

'Like what?' She poured herself coffee.

'Like, for starters, how did you meet him?'

'Through *Cyrano Inc.*' Rosie could have bitten off her tongue.

'*He's* one of the dating-impaired. I don't believe it.'

'It's a long story.' And Rosie wasn't about to tell it. Not only would she have to field a barrage of I-told-you-so's from Jonesy; she'd be violating Kent's confidence.

'So what's my accounting crisis of the week?' Rosie asked, deciding her best course was a change of subject.

Jonesy ignored her. 'You're infatuated.'

Jonesy didn't believe in love, so Rosie guessed this was the best description she could come up with. 'Nope. I'm in lust. Nothing more and nothing less.'

'So.'

'So, what?'

'So, this is great news. This is what you want. Right?'

'I want lust?'

'It's the usual jumping-off point.'

'Not for me.'

'Rosaleen, are you crazy? The man's spectacular. He's a partner in a thriving business—in a growth sector of the economy—has a solid work ethic, owns his own home, and has well-laid plans for his future.'

Rosie's mouth fell open. 'You got all that in twenty minutes?'

'Just tell me. What can possibly be wrong?'

'Not a thing. He's perfect for you, Jonesy. Go for it.'

'Are you serious?' Her eyes narrowed in speculation.

'No, I'm not. Touch him and you're dead meat.'

Jonesy smirked. 'I thought so.'

Rosie turned her coffee cup and stared at the delicate flowers painted around its base. 'He doesn't like kids, Jonesy. I may lust after a man who doesn't like kids, but I could never love one.'

*　　　*　　　*

Kent sat in the car and watched rain course down the windshield. He was thirty feet from the door of the club, but he couldn't make himself open the car door.

And what the hell had made him drive right past Beachline and land on Rosie's doorstep? He might as well have been on autopilot. That bit about his misplacing his scheduler was a crock. He'd wanted to see her. Had to see her. It was as simple as that.

Not simple at all.

The woman was a fertility goddess in training. He shuddered. Kids. She wanted kids, a whole scout troop of them. And she'd used them like garlic on vampire to ward him off. He admitted she'd been fair—and right. So why had he spent the whole weekend thinking about her? He had no intention of overworking a stork. They were about ten kids apart and would probably stay that way.

Unless . . .

Marlene rapped on the window. He opened it, and the damp air invaded the car like a sodden wind. 'Kent, what are you doing sitting out here? Are you okay?'

She peered at him from under a huge golf umbrella. 'Yeah, just thinking.' And working up a Machiavellian plot to change a certain

77

lady's mind about a bearing a child for every sign in the zodiac. He'd be doing her a favor. One good look at her 'plan' in living, breathing color, and she'd backtrack faster than a tourist faced with a grizzly.

Marlene stepped back and he opened the door.

'Packard's waiting. He's threatening to walk off the project if you initiate the penalty clause.'

She lifted the umbrella to accomodate his height, and he stepped under. 'Let's go.' He took Marlene's arm and headed for the door. Packard he could handle. Rosie he wasn't so sure of.

The meeting with Packard took less than half an hour, ending with his agreement to add more manpower and swallow some overtime costs. If he kept to his word, everything would be smooth sailing from here on in.

When he got back to his office, the first thing he did was rifle through his mail. Nothing from the mysterious Gardenia. And for the first time, he was disappointed.

He wasn't disappointed by his phone messages. Rosie had called. He picked up the phone and hammered in her number.

'Rosie?'

'Hey, Summerton, I just wanted to say thanks for the home remedy. It helped. I'm feeling better.'

'I'm glad.'

'In fact I felt good enough to crack open the Beachline manual. I've already got some questions and was wondering if I could call your pro shop. That's who manages tee times, right?'

'Right. But I'm sure I can answer most of them. Try me.'

'Actually, I'd rather talk to the golf pro and the people who deal with the golfers on a day-to-day basis. If that's okay?'

'Sure, I'll let them know you'll be calling.' He paused. 'You know, it would be a good idea if you met the people here, got a feel for the place. Why don't I pick you up tomorrow—say around eleven. After you've made the rounds, I'll take you to lunch.'

For a moment she was silent.

'Strictly business, right?' she said.

'Absolutely. You think I want to get myself tangled up with a woman who plans to spend the rest of her life in a delivery room?'

Another brief pause. 'No. I don't think you do. Eleven will be fine.'

He hung up, feeling smug. The plan—*his* plan—was in motion.

*   *   *

Rosie shoved a wayward tendril of hair behind her ear and watched Kent turn into her driveway. Font imitated a growl and glanced up at her. When she shook her head to tell him that guard dog duty wasn't called for, he lined up his gaze to match hers. Together they watched Kent Summerton drive the gravel path to the house, the sunlight bouncing off the polish of his high-powered car.

She waved and ignored the wobble in her knees, those rubbery muscles in her calves.

The car crunched up to the bottom step, and she started down.

'Are you always so prompt?' she asked, after he'd opened the door for her and she'd settled in the car.

'A failing.'

'Me, too.'

He glanced at her and put the car in gear. His look was disbelieving, but he grinned. And naturally she went all quivery inside. And naturally it made her mad as heck.

'I *was* standing on the step waiting, or didn't you notice?' Even to her own ear she sounded nicely bitchy and proudly chagrined. She'd always wanted to be chagrined. She hoped it impressed him.

'I'd notice you if you were standing in Times Square on New Year's eve, O'Hanlon. I think we both know that.'

That shut her up. She settled for silence until they were nearing Beachline and he started to tell her about the people she was going to meet.

Inside the club's impressive doors they were met by a frosted cookie named Marlene, who looked at Rosie as if she were a soggy-mouthed rottweiler with one of Marlene's three hundred dollar Italian pumps clasped in her teeth. The pump, Rosie guessed, was Kent Summerton.

They shook hands with the showy enthusiasm of two rival politicians at a joint fundraising.

'Kent, I've been waiting for you,' Marlene said, turning to Kent. 'Con called. He said if you phone before eleven-thirty you can catch him at his hotel.' She looked at her watch. 'You've got five minutes.'

Kent's expression hardened. 'You'll have to excuse me, Rosie.'

'No problem. I'm sure Marlene can point me in the right direction.'

'Marlene, how about starting Rosie off in accounting? Introduce her to Susan. I'll catch up with you there.'

Marlene nodded. She and Rosie moved toward the lair of bean counters and computers as Kent strode off, double time, in the opposite direction.

Marlene and Rosie smiled at each other, showing enough straight, gleaming teeth to make a crocodile writhe in envy.

'How nice of you to make time to come and see us,' Marlene said, not meaning a word of it.

'Nice to be here,' Rosie said, then she giggled.

Marlene gave her a puzzled look.

'Sorry, I was just thinking how wonderfully vague the word "nice" is. How it's so often used to say the exact opposite of what it means.'

They stopped outside a door with a sign saying STAFF ONLY, and Marlene's smile fell from her face like snow from a tin roof. 'Are you saying I'm insincere?'

'Uh-huh. But that's okay. If I had my cap set for Kent Summerton, I'd be leery of me, too.'

'I don't know what you're talking about.'

'I think you do.'

Marlene started to say something, then stopped. A tight smile bowed her lips. 'I've got a flash for you, Miss O'Hanlon. Every woman in the place has her "cap" set for Kent Summerton.'

'But?' Rosie tilted her head. 'There's a but in there somewhere. I can smell it.'

'*But* it seems Kent has an aversion to "caps" regardless of what woman's head it sits on. The only thing that turns him on is work, work, and more work.'

'I know.' Rosie sighed noisily. 'And it is, as they say, a cryin' shame. All that good husband material going to waste.'

Marlene gave her a searching look, then laughed. 'You, too, huh?' She shrugged. 'Well, all I can tell you is the line forms to the right, and it's damn long.' She pushed open the door a couple of inches, then stopped. 'You're all right, Rosie. It'll be fun working with you.'

Rosie put out her hand, and Marlene took it. They both chuckled. 'Lead on, Marlene. Nothing like the warmth and charm of a well-run accounting department to make me feel at home.'

*　　*　　*

By the time Kent joined them, Marlene, Susan Lyle, and Rosie were sitting in Susan's office drinking coffee and laughing like schoolgirls. Actually, it sounded more like giggling. Not that any man in his right mind would accuse them of that. He was pretty sure women didn't 'giggle' any more. When he stepped into the office, Susan, always shy and hesitant around him, sobered immediately and began fussing with the papers on her desk. He glanced past her to the clock behind her desk. Twelve-ten.

'Rosie, I promised you lunch. Are you done here?' If he read it right, they'd barely got started. At this rate it would take Rosie forever to finish this project, which was just fine with him. He'd take all the time with her he could get.

'Yes, and I'm starved.' She stood, then turned back to Susan and Marlene. 'When I'm finished with the manual, we'll celebrate, okay? Have dinner at my place and finish dissecting the inner workings of the opposite sex.'

'We'll be there,' Marlene said, answering for Susan.

'Oh, and Marlene? I should have the first pages for you Friday. I'll send the file through e-mail.'

*   *   *

In the dining room, Kent pulled out Rosie's chair and she settled in, looking both preoccupied and pleased with herself.

Within seconds Mae Smythe, Beachline's newest server, was at their table, smiling broadly, telling them the specials, and leaving menus. Inwardly, Kent groaned. If he'd hoped for privacy with Rosie, that hope was lost with Mae waiting their table. He knew from experience she'd be filling his water glass every five seconds.

'Good meeting?' Kent asked, setting aside the menu he could have recited in his sleep.

Rosie looked up. 'Excellent. I like your people. Marlene's amazing. There isn't anything she doesn't know about this place. And Susan . . . Well, let's just say I think her DNA would show she's Jonesy's long-lost twin. Neat lady.'

'Yes, they're both valuable Beachline employees, very committed to their careers.'

Rosie lifted her eyes to meet his directly, their expression impish. 'Not like some misguided women you know. Right,

Summerton?'

'That's not—'

'May I take your order?'

Mae, accompanied by the clinking ice cubes in her water pitcher, arrived to hover over Kent's shoulder. He put his hand over his glass and nodded in Rosie's direction. Mae gave her a bright smile. After Rosie had her explain the ingredients that made the chicken special so special, they ordered.

'I'm not misguided, you know,' Rosie said, turning her attention back to him. 'I know exactly what I want, just as Marlene and Susan do. And I'm equally as committed to it.'

He loved her eyes, so wide and honest, not a hint of subterfuge or guile. He'd never looked into eyes so blue, so filled with humor. He noticed then.

'Your glasses are fixed.'

She touched the lower rim, then shot him an irritated look. 'You're not listening again, Summerton. I was talking about my commitment.'

'I know, but when did you get your glasses repaired?'

She rolled her eyes. 'Saturday. Hennessy came and took me to the optometrist.' She pierced him with a look. 'Happy now?'

'You should have called me. I would have taken you.'

'Are you crazy? Why would I call you?'

'Why did you call Hennessy?'

'Because he's my friend.'

'So, what am I?'

Her lips moved, but nothing came out. 'Good question, Summerton. A very good question.'

'And one I'd like an answer to.'

'You're a recent acquaintance.'

'That's it?'

She looked at him as though he were in full military gear with a sack of land mines strapped to his back. The lady was cautious.

'Okay, let's see.' She fiddled with her fork, then aligned it perfectly with her plate before looking at him. 'You're an acquaintance, a customer of MooreWrite, a man I'm trying to extricate from an over-heated and over-avid woman's attentions, a single guy who'd love to have a no-strings affair, and a highly developed peptic ulcer waiting to perforate.'

He laughed. 'I don't have an ulcer.'

She smiled serenely. 'You will, Summerton. You will. Then she added, 'I notice you didn't deny the "no-strings affair" part of my description.'

'Can't.'

She sipped her water. 'You're honest, anyway. I guess that's something.' The way she said it, it didn't sound like much. Maybe on a par with putting the toilet seat down. But the damn truth was he didn't know what he wanted from Rosie—other than a repeat of that sizzling kitchen kiss.

Mae brought their orders and for the remainder of their lunch, they stuck to neutral subjects. They weathered it with only six interruptions, not all of them from Mae.

After lunch they were walking toward the pro shop, when Rosie asked, 'Is it always like that? So many people coming at you for things?'

'It's a bit worse than usual. My partner's away.' Enough said. Right now, he didn't want to think about Con York, let alone tell Rosie about him. Con's recent penchant for playing hookey was beginning to wear thin. It hadn't started out that way. At first they'd worked together, but lately Kent had taken over virtually all of Con's work. He was beginning to feel like a fool for tying up with him in the first place.

He opened the door to the pro shop and followed Rosie in. Greg was waiting for them.

'Rosie, this is Greg Nestor. He's our golf professional. Between him and Marlene, I think you can find the answers to all your questions.' When he looked down at her, he caught the faint scent of lemons. Knowing Rosie, a man couldn't be sure if it was perfume or pie ingredient. 'When you're finished here, let me know. I'll drive you home.'

She pushed her chin against the brace in what passed for a nod and, unless he read her wrong, had just a little trouble pulling her gaze from his. His breathing warmed, and he concentrated on his own problem, shifting his eyes to look at Greg. 'Take care of the lady, Greg,' he said, his voice odd to his own ears. 'I'll be in my office.'

He had arrangements to make for a family barbecue. It was show-and-tell time.

*   *   *

Rosie called Kent at three to tell him she'd done all she was going to do for today, and by three-thirty they were in his car. Rosie was tired, but she was determined it wouldn't show. This was the longest time she been away from home since her surgery. All she wanted to do was go home and put her head down. But she couldn't. Not yet.

She glanced at Kent. The lines in his forehead were drawn tight enough to snap. She resisted the urge to smooth them away. No. It would be all too easy to make Kent Summerton and his stress lines a full-time job. She stilled her twitchy fingers.

'Kent, would you drop me off on Yates Street? I've got a doctor's appointment at four.'

'No problem.' He started the car.

'Thanks.' She smiled, not wanting him to see her own weariness.

'How are you getting home?' he asked.

'Hennessy's picking me up.'

'No, he isn't.'

'Excuse me?'

'I'll take you to the doctor, and I'll wait.'

CHAPTER SIX

'But I told Hennessy I'd call when I was done. He's expecting to hear from me.'

'I'll call him.'

The set of his chin said argument was futile. 'Fine,' she agreed. 'If you want to play taxi driver, so be it.'

She was grumpy about it and let it show. She didn't know what Kent Summerton had in mind, and it bugged her. She hoped he wasn't the kind of guy who took the word no as a challenge, because she wasn't sure she was up for it. Her blood simmered every time she laid eyes on him; a roiling boil was a distinct threat. Even her current state of exhaustion didn't make her immune. All she had left was her willpower. Now there was a scary thought.

She left him sitting in the doctor's reception area with his nose in a copy of *Fortune Magazine*. Of course she got all mushy and flickery inside, thinking he looked like an expectant father waiting for a newly pregnant wife. Hopeless, she was hopeless.

'You're doing great, Rosie,' Dr. Winters said. 'You'll be out of the brace in no time at all.' He walked with her to the reception area

89

where Kent waited. 'Until then, continue to take it easy and don't do anything foolish—and stop looking at me like that,' he added, giving her a stern look. 'I didn't promise anything. That surgery you had was no joke, young lady. I'm not about to have all my hard work undone because you can't wait to go bungee jumping . . .'

'I know, but I was hoping the darn thing could at least be downgraded from steel to latex. I'm a bit tired of being a human lightning rod.' She smiled through her disappointment. She really had hoped she'd be able to talk him into taking the damn thing off today.

Feeling unrepentantly sorry for herself, she walked over to where Kent sat waiting. He looked up and smiled. 'Something looks different,' he said, nodding at her neckwear.

'I had a tune-up. He lowered it a bit.'

He stood, then leaned down to plant a brief kiss just to the left of her mouth. 'It must feel better,' he added, holding her by the shoulders and studying her updated hydraulics.

What felt good were his lips grazing hers, the hum of his deep voice in her ear, the scent of him tickling her nose. She had the insane urge to wrap her arms around him and ask for a hug. And more kisses, definitely more kisses. She wanted to feel like a woman again instead of a space needle spin-off. She wanted to be cuddled, and then some.

In the car, he turned to her, his green eyes questioning and intent. 'Anything else you need to do before going home? Anywhere else you want to go?'

How about the nearest motel with clean sheets? Hormone leered, snapping a lace-fringed garter. Troublemaker.

'No, just home,' she said, emphatically enough for him to give her a puzzled glance. Rosie settled back in the car and sent an SOS to Lady Brain. She arrived brandishing a full color set of baby pictures. Triplets. Rosie concentrated on naming them during the ride home. Kent picked up his cellullar phone and started talking to Marlene about a man called Packard and a barbecue.

Rosie, now able to turn her head without swiveling her upper body, kept stealing peeks at him, admiring his knuckles; one set curved around the phone, the other on the steering wheel. She studied how he compressed his lips on one side of his mouth when he was thinking. She noticed how decisively he drove, the way he dipped his head to look in the rear view mirror instead of adjusting it. She noticed everything she could and imagined the rest.

She wondered if he could hear the sigh curling around her heart and nudging her stomach, if he could sense her difficulty in drawing all but the shallowest of breaths? Rosie couldn't remember this kind of wanting. Ever.

In less than forty minutes they were pulling into her yard, and in that same time Rosie's imagination had them upstairs tangled in her country-rose sheets. With no trouble at all, she'd cranked the heat from simmer to pre-boil.

Rosie hesitated, but only for half a nanosecond, then said, 'Want to come in for a while?' Her mouth was dry and her heart pounded like a drum. Every wayward nerve in her body jangled.

Kent turned his full attention on her. He was reading her mind, she just knew it. She forced a smile.

Then Summerton made the perfect move.

He glanced at his watch.

The hot tide of passion engulfing Rosie seemed to disappear. Lady Brain took over in one big hurry.

Rosie exhaled the remainder of her self-manufactured heat, and said, 'Then again, maybe not. I'm tired. I think I'll just go in and stretch out.'

Kent turned the car off and, one arm draped over the steering wheel, turned to study her, his gaze thoughtful. Finally, he nodded. 'Good idea. I've got a dinner meeting. We wouldn't have nearly enough time to do it right.'

'Do what right?' She had no doubt his 'it' and her 'it' were two different species.

Summerton smiled. 'Make love. That is

what's on your mind, isn't it?'

'Excuse me?' Haughty. She needed to be haughty here. She gave it her best shot, and figured she carried it off.

Kent tilted his head but didn't move. 'Come here, Red. That brace isn't going to stop me.'

She looked at him, his gaze set on her as if she were a chocolate cake and he was icing. The man was a macho, arrogant, smug, overconfident, presumptuous, egotistical—

'Red?'

'Do you have any idea how outraged I am?'

He didn't shift a bone or stretch a sinew. He just sat and waited.

'You really, honestly think I'm going to fall into your arms like a needy, sex-deprived female who hasn't a brain in her head?'

'A guy can hope,' he said, grinning.

She didn't intend to laugh. She truly didn't. The damn sound just came out of her mouth. She tried to smother her laugh with a cough. It didn't work.

Kent moved toward her, ran a finger down her arm, his grin gone. 'I'm the needy one here, Rosie,' he said, his voice low and serious.

She shot him a glance.

He tugged on her arm, not a demand, a request.

Hormone accepted on her behalf.

He pulled her close, gently, and moved his mouth over hers in a kiss so soft it was invisible, except to her heart. He pulled his head back, looked down at her and stroked a thumb across her lower lip. 'This is getting serious, you know. Eating home-cooked meals together. Working together. Going to the doctor together.' One corner of his mouth quirked up. 'Putting our mouths together.'

'It's not serious, Summerton. Trust me on that.' Why didn't the man get on with it and kiss her? Really kiss her. He was making her crazy. Her chest felt as though someone was in there inflating a balloon. Her vision was blurred, except for Kent's face, which was in perfect focus. Her mind she kept closed. She didn't want to hear about getting serious.

He touched her lips again, then replaced his thumb with his mouth. Then he turned up the heat. Rosie had never felt lips like Kent's, firm and gentle, cool and heat streaked, taking and giving. Her hands splayed across the muscles of his chest then, when his tongue touched hers, clutched the cotton of his shirt. She heard him groan softly, felt the beat of his heart against her knuckles, then her own against the back of her hand, before sliding her arms around his neck. Oh, yes, those tangled sheets were definitely in the works. His hand rested just under her breast, and she shifted, wanting him to cup her fully. Wanting more than that.

'Rosie?' Kent shuddered, and a rush of breath warmed her throat. He gripped her shoulders, set her back from him. 'Can we take this up later?' he said, his breath ragged, his eyes hot.

She blinked, tried to focus. What was he saying? Something about later? She blinked again.

'Rosie, I've got to go. I've got a date, and the lady is special.'

The word *date*, coupled with *lady*, got her full attention.

Still holding her, he leaned his forehead against hers. 'I don't want to go, I *have* to go.'

With her new neckwear, she could lift her chin, so she did. 'You're a piece of work, Summerton, you really are. First, you kiss me senseless, and in the next breath you tell me you have a date. A damned date, for heaven's sake.'

'Did I really?'

'Really, what?' she grumped, stuffing her feet in her shoes and trying to remember when they came off.

'Kiss you senseless?'

She rolled her eyes. 'Now the man wants a testimonial.' He laughed. 'It's my mother, O'Hanlon. I've got a date with my mother. Can I be excused?'

'Your mother?'

He leaned back but continued to run a finger lazily up and down her forearm. 'Every year my family gets together for a barbecue. It's a rotating host arrangement, and this year it's my turn. Mother's determined to hover this year. Ensure that I do my bit, even though the Beachline staff will be doing the work for me.' He continued to play with her hair. 'It's a week from Saturday. Will you come?'

'To the barbecue?'

He nodded.

'With you?'

He nodded again.

'Sounds like a date to me.' This last she said more to herself than to Kent, turning his question over in her mind as if it were a beach rock, fully expecting to find some unsavory creature lurking beneath with teeth at the ready. She tugged at her hair, but as usual common sense was AWOL.

'Come with me,' he urged.

'What about my kids?'

'What kids?'

'The ones I told you about. I haven't changed my mind. I want a big—make that very big—family.'

'I asked you to come to a barbecue, Rosie, not a sterilization clinic.'

'You asked me to meet your mother, Summerton. There are those of us of the female persuasion who might read something into that.' That ought to put the run on him.

'True,' he said. 'But you're not one of them, so I have nothing to worry about.'

He smiled then, lifted his wrist, and again looked at his watch, shaking his head regretfully. 'Speaking of mothers, if I know mine, she's already waiting in my office.' He leaned forward and brushed his lips across hers. 'Then again, maybe Marlene can entertain her awhile longer.'

When he reached for her, Rosie reached for her bag, then opened the car door. 'Good boys don't keep their moms waiting.'

She was half out of the car when she heard him say, 'I think I've been a good boy long enough.'

She was nearly to her front door when she heard him yell from the car window. 'Rosie! Will you come to the barbecue?'

She turned. 'I'll think about it, but that doesn't mean I want to have sex with you, Summerton.' Now why on earth did she say that? Doctor Winters should do her a favor and put a few screws in her mouth.

He grinned and waved. 'And I'll take that as a yes—on both counts.'

*   *   *

Kent listened intently to his mother's plan for the Summerton family barbecue. It was obvious she wasn't leaving much of the planning or organizing up to him. She'd made up notes for him, for God's sake. After her in-depth review of them, she shoved them across his desk.

'You won't forget Uncle Albert is on a special diet—' she gestured with her head

97

toward the list in his hand '—and Evie and George aren't eating meat?'

'I got it. And you're sure everyone— absolutely *everyone* is coming?'

She beamed. 'Not a no-show in the bunch.'

Kent matched her smile. 'Let's see then, including uncles, aunts, cousins, and assorted others. That makes sixty-eight adults and—' his smile widened '—forty kids between the ages of one and thirteen.'

'Forty-one, if you count Josh.'

'Josh?' Kent said vacantly, knowing he was losing track. At the rate his family was reproducing he needed a computer to keep track.

'Claire and Jimmy's latest?'

'I thought they called him Joe.'

'They changed their minds.'

'Ah,' was about all he could say to that. 'I think we can leave baby Josh out of the count. But if you think of anything else, call and I'll make sure the club takes care of it.' This was one occasion when Kent was damn glad he managed a resort with a large outdoor entertainment area. Anything less than a golf course would be seriously inadequate.

Mary Summerton, who'd been sitting in the seat on the other side of Kent's desk, stood to go. 'That's it then, love. I've got to run. Your father's at Mike's helping him build a barbecue pit, and I'm supposed to meet him there. We're going out to dinner.'

Kent stood and walked around his desk to where she stood. 'I'm disappointed. I was hoping we could have dinner together. Mike has all the luck.' He smiled. Mike was one of Kent's four brothers.

She looked surprised. 'Why didn't you say something, dear? I would have loved that. I just assumed you'd be too busy.'

'And I assumed you'd be available.' He kissed her forehead, genuinely regretful. It occurred to him he hadn't sat down and talked with either of his parents in a long time. He missed it. 'Looks like we were both wrong. Next time then.'

'Absolutely.' She hugged him. 'And if you need anymore help with the reunion, you let me know.'

'It may never be the same after its first Summerton invasion, but I'm sure Beachline will handle it.'

She gave him a speculative look. 'You're surprisingly obliging about all this, Kent. Is there something I'm missing here?'

'Uh-uh. Just doing my bit for the Summerton clan.' And preparing to show a certain woman what having a too-large family is really all about. If seeing forty wild kids and their frazzled relatives and parents in action didn't do it, nothing would.

His mother eyed him with a glint of speculation. 'You're bringing someone, aren't you?'

Kent felt his jaw loosen. He'd forgotten his mother's uncanny ability to read his mind—along with those of his four brothers and five sisters.

He wouldn't lie to her. 'Yes—' he said, breaking off when her smile threatened to encompass her entire face. He held up his hands. 'But it's not anything serious, so don't start booking the hall.' He kissed her again and opened his office door. 'Have a nice dinner, Mom.'

She was still smiling when she turned to wave good-bye. Mothers were incorrigible romantics. A guy might as well accept it. And he wasn't sure he was telling the whole truth. Something was 'serious' between O'Hanlon and him, or at least could be if the woman could be brought around to thinking in terms of an adult relationship instead of a kindergarten.

Something in his gut—and lower—wanted to pursue *something* with Rosie, but the bare truth was she was right about his attitude toward having a houseful of kids. His own house had shook, bulged, and groaned under the stress. The youngest of the bunch, he'd envied his friends their orderly dinner tables, their own rooms, their privacy. As the last one in, he'd been the Johnny-come-lately, the runt nudged constantly toward the back. He didn't blame his parents. They were the best, but by the time he showed up, the crowd around them was so big he was lost in it. Chaos ruled.

Rosie had no idea what she was in for, but if he could show her, she might do a one-eighty. He had to hope, because he was smart enough to know you didn't mess with maternal instinct. If Rosie didn't adjust her own thinking, he sure as hell wasn't going to try and argue her into it—or let himself get further involved.

*   *   *

Rosie woke with a start. When her eyes popped open, she closed them quickly, determined to hold the remnants of her dream behind her eyelids. Not a dream really. A realization. Yesterday, at Beachline, she'd heard a familiar voice. Gardenia's voice. She was sure of it. In her dream the voice had a face, but now, no matter how she tried to hold it, the dream was escaping her. The face was gone and the voice was fading.

She lined up the Beachline staff she'd met in her head. Marlene, Susan, Mae, and what's-her-name in the pro shop. She scrunched her brow and tugged hard at the tail end of the dream. Her eyelids started to hurt.

Useless. It was useless.

She sat up and opened her eyes, letting the last of the dream drift away. She threw back the covers and sat on the edge of the bed.

For now she'd leave it alone. No sense

calling Kent and alarming him about his staff. It was only a dream, after all. But at least now she had a plan B. If her letter to Gardenia didn't work, she'd spend more time around Beachline. If Gardenia did work there, she'd identify the voice and that would be that. She pushed up from the bed and stretched, then poked at the seemingly dead dog stretched out beside her bed. He groaned a complaint.

'Up, you useless hound,' she said, scratching his ear. 'We've got work to do, and we're going underground to do it.'

She had bills to pay, and a manual to compose. For the next week or so, she wasn't going to think about Gardenia, dreams, barbecues, or Kent Summerton.

The Summerton family barbecue. She could just imagine it. A half dozen people eating filet mignon on the Beachline patio, while insects fried themselves on the bug light. She probably wouldn't go, but of course she couldn't be sure. When it came to Kent Summerton, she seemed to be doing a lot of things she hadn't planned on doing.

He shouldn't have kissed her. It wasn't fair. She couldn't think rationally when he kissed her. But then, she didn't think rationally most of the time. Except about filling her life with kids. That wasn't a whim. It was her calling, a vocation, a primal and wondrous need. And no one—not even Summerton with his hot, passionate kisses—was going to mess with it.

And she'd better get on it. In no time her brace would be history, and she'd start dating again. Ugh. Odd, she'd been so looking forward to it—until Kent had come into her life.

Yup. Incommunicado, that was the ticket. A few days to work hard, straighten out her head, and prioritize stuff.

She headed to the bathroom, frowning. Prioritize. Had she actually used that word? Obviously she'd been hanging out with the wrong people.

*   *   *

Kent hadn't seen Rosie in over a week. He'd called several times and all he got was her voice message saying, 'I left last night on the last train to Borneo. Will be gone until I return. Further attempts to communicate will be futile unless you have a working set of jungle drums. Do not call, fax, or e-mail until further notice.'

Kent had done all three, persistently to no avail.

He swiveled his chair to face the window, idly turning his pen between thumb and index finger. It was a dismal Monday morning; sun shining, birds singing, golfers swinging—and over ten days since he'd seen her. It had taken a lot less time than that for him to admit he missed her. O'Hanlon was under his skin.

Deep. Funny thing was he didn't mind. Didn't mind at all.

He knew she was working on the Beachline manual, because Greg had heard from her, as had Susan and Marlene. But she hadn't called him, not even to say she was, or was not, coming to the barbecue. Not that he had any intention of letting her out of it.

That decision made, he turned back to his desk. Time to get to work. He hadn't heard anyone come in, but a new stack of mail formed a silo on his desk. He hadn't heard from his pen pal since Rosie mailed her letter, but unless he was wrong, that was the scent of Gardenia drifting up his nose. He rifled the pile and smiled when he spotted the pale pink envelope. He put his feet up on his desk and opened the letter.

Sleep brings dreams of you, my tiger.
Come dream with me.
See what I see, feel what I feel
Our mouths joined at last.
Skin to skin.
Our bodies moist, blazing with a dark,
* wild heat.*
My naked, aching breasts hard against your
* chest.*
I want you, Kent. I crave your hot, hard
* length.*
In love and longing,
                                          Gardenia

Kent shifted in his chair.

Rosie's purple prose made his own thoughts *decidedly* blue. And they had nothing to do with Gardenia and a hell of a lot to do with the vision of being skin-to-skin with Rosie O'Hanlon.

He slapped the letter on his desk and exhaled as if he'd run a marathon.

Then he noticed the hand-printed note on the back of the letter. 'I received *Cyrano*'s message, Tiger, but I know you don't really want me to stop writing. My courage is growing, so we'll meet soon. I will be naked and waiting—where you least expect me.'

'S——!' Kent straightened. He picked up the phone to call Rosie, then remembered her recent trip to Borneo. Tonight. He'd go out to her place tonight. This was one development she had to hear about.

*   *   *

'I'm not here.' Rosie yelled for the third time, determined to get through to the idiot banging on her door. She gave a beseeching glance to Font who was sleeping in the middle of the doorway. No help from that quarter. The banging continued. She sighed and headed for the door. It was past eight and time to quit, anyway, not to mention she was starved. It was probably only Jonesy bursting with the financial crisis of the week. They could share some soup.

'Summerton, what are you doing here? I told you, I'm in Borneo.' Her hand shot to the wildness she called hair. She must look as if she'd been standing around with her finger in an electrical socket. When was the last time she looked in a mirror? Yesterday? The day before? And here was Summerton, looking as though he'd just leapt freshly ironed from the cover of *GQ*. Irritated with the unfairness of it, she plucked a paper clip from her mane of glory and let him stand there.

After a moment of silence, he asked, 'Can I come in?'

'No.'

'No,' he repeated, then waved a sheet of rose linen stationery in her face. 'This from a woman who lusts after the "long, hard length" of me?'

She snatched the paper from his hand. 'Damn!' she said, turning and walking back into the house. Kent followed, until they both arrived in her kitchen. 'Enough time had passed. I figured my letter had done the trick.' She slapped the offending paper against her thigh.

'Look at the back.'

She turned the letter over. 'Damn,' she said again, then sighed. She'd have to tell him her suspicions about one of his staff. Too bad her dream wasn't more specific. He'd think she was a gold-plated flake, but it couldn't be helped.

She went to the fridge and took out some salad greens, then went to the stove and turned the heat on under the soup.

'What are you doing?' Kent stood by the unlit fireplace frowning.

'I'm thinking and making myself something to eat. And unless I miss my guess, you just left the club where you had to miss lunch due to an emergency meeting and so haven't eaten a thing since breakfast.'

He grinned.

She rolled her eyes.

'Wait,' he said, taking off his jacket and striding over to the cooking island, 'I'll do the salad thing, you stir the soup—and think.'

*　　　*　　　*

Rosie munched on the last crust of her bread while Kent cleared the table. She thought idly that some woman, at sometime in Kent's life, had done a pretty good job of basic training. Then she folded her napkin. Might as well get this over with.

'Kent.'

'Uh-huh.' He came back and joined her at the table, bringing two cups of coffee.

'I think Gardenia works for you.'

'No way. I know all the women at Beachline. Not one of them gives me a second thought—

other than at salary review time.' He thought for a moment, shook his head, and repeated firmly. 'No way.'

She stared at him, and said nothing. Lord, was he that unaware? The women at Beachline almost bumped into walls when he walked down the hall.

'You're not serious,' he said. 'You can't be.'

'I'm very serious. I think I heard her voice when I was there.'

'You think? Why didn't you say something then?'

She hesitated, twirled a strand of hair. 'Because it kind of, uh, came to me in a dream a couple of days later.'

'A dream.' He leaned back in his chair, looking at her as if she'd just admitted to spotting Elvis at the local coin laundry. 'I see.'

She glanced skyward, trying to ignore his insufferable tone of voice. 'Yes, a dream,' she said firmly, with a fine lift of her chin. 'And if you patronize me, Summerton, the next meal you have here will be laced with rat poison.'

His lips quirked up at the corners. 'Glad to know they'll be a next time. Rat poison or not.'

The man was quick. Too quick. She glared at him.

'So tell me about this dream,' he said in velvet tones, sounding like an oh-so-patient psychiatrist about to probe the psyche of a deranged mental patient.

She was sure she had rat poison around

108

here somewhere.

CHAPTER SEVEN

Kent listened to Rosie intently as she told him about her dream. If it hadn't included a witches' coven, a green-eyed shapeshifter, and a magic fog, he might be less skeptical. He'd never put any stock in dreams, and after listening to Rosie's, he knew why. But he wasn't about to tell her that.

She insisted that one of her dream-witches was Gardenia. She'd caught a glimpse of her face under a white hood, she told him earnestly—which apparently implied she was a good witch.

Okay . . .

'But you can't actually identify which of the witches sounded like Gardenia?' he asked in as sober a voice as he could muster.

Rosie shook her head. 'No. And it's been driving me nuts. It could be one of the women in accounting. I don't think it's Marlene, but then . . . Oh, I don't know—' She combed her hands through her hair from the temples out, grimacing when she unearthed another paper clip. She twisted it idly before adding, 'As for the others, I'm not sure. But I heard Gardenia's voice, I'm sure of it. And I'm almost certain it was at Beachline.'

'Almost certain?' he repeated, his face tight from keeping it straight. Rosie might not have identified Gardenia, but she had given him an opportunity. He decided to take it. The trick was to remain cool and work his plan. He stood. 'If you want to check out this dream angle, you'll have to come back to Beachline. Spend more time there.' He removed his jacket from the chair back and shrugged into it. 'Next Saturday will be perfect.'

'Why next Saturday?' She looked doubtful.

'We're hosting a special event. Everyone you met when you were there last will be on the premises.' He didn't bother to mention they'd also be there the four days prior to Saturday—or that the 'special event' was the Summerton family barbecue. This way, if she turned down his request to go to the barbecue with him, he had an ace in the hole. He walked toward the door, and she walked with him, silent, still fiddling with the paper clip. At the door she looked up at him.

'You don't believe in my dream, do you?' she said, looking uncertain and challenging at the same time.

'I don't believe Gardenia is one of Beachline's employees, but if you can prove me wrong . . .'

Her eyes narrowed, then lit with determination. 'My pleasure, Summerton,' she said.

'And this is mine.' He gripped her shoulders

110

and pulled her close enough to catch a whiff of vanilla and feel her breath on his neck. He kissed her the way he'd been wanting to for days now. And God, if the woman didn't tuck into his arms as though she'd been wanting the same damn thing, folding into him as though she were coming home. Her mouth was so soft, so giving, his orderly thoughts and plans went south in a hurry. He didn't want to let her go. Ever.

'Oh, Kent,' she whispered, propping her braced head against his chest. 'You're making me crazy.'

He lifted her head, brushed his lips over hers. 'That's the idea, O'Hanlon.' He kissed her chin, her cheek, her ear, her wild hair.

She giggled. 'Be careful there, hotshot, I'm not sure I got all the paperclips out.' She pulled away, gazing at him with a terrifically wistful expression, then pushed hard at his chest. 'Go. Before I forget myself and start ripping your shirt off.'

'Hell of an idea.'

She smiled and he smiled back, then he smoothed her hair away from her forehead, kissed its warm, smooth skin. Briefly, he considered pushing his advantage, but decided against it. He didn't want either of them to do something they'd regret. When he and Rosie went to bed together—and they would—he wanted her to want it as much as he did. No reservations. No misunderstandings. After

Saturday and a clearheaded view of what a big. family *really* meant, a consensus between them was inevitable. If economic arguments couldn't change her mind, maybe the sight of a few dozen sticky-faced kids and a batch of worn-out parents would.

He stepped back and opened the door. 'Saturday then? Say about noon? I'll pick you up.'

'Okay.'

He was opening his car door, when she called to him from the top step. 'Kent, about the barbecue? I'm sorry, but I'm not going. It wouldn't be a good idea. I meant what I said about, uh, us. There's just no way . . .'

'You're probably right,' he said, trying to keep his face straight.

'And Kent? I can't stay too late on Saturday. My neck brace is coming off Friday, and I've joined a single's club. There's a dance that night, and I've already been paired up.'

Paired up . . .

Kent's smile crashed and burned, right along with his smug attitude.

*   *   *

'Mae, would you bring me a thermos of coffee from the kitchen?' Kent asked, slapping a two-inch sheaf of papers on his desk and taking his seat. 'I'm going to be here awhile.'

'Sure.' Mae said, picking up his cold coffee

112

and adding it to her tray. 'Can I bring you something to eat?'

'No, thanks,' Kent mumbled, trying to focus on the financial reports in front of him. He heard a click when the door closed. And the click set his mind wandering—again. A singles dance. What in hell was wrong with the woman?

What had she said? 'Paired up.' Over his dead body.

Now he was on a deadline, dictated to by a damn neck brace. He cursed, and rubbed at the irritation lodged in his forehead.

He *could* just let the universe unfold as Rosie wanted it. That would be the fairest thing to do. But fair was the last thing on his mind. He wanted her, and not just in bed. That thought stuck and held too long for comfort. He couldn't deny it; he was falling big time for Rosie O'Hanlon, but, damn it, he did *not* want to set off a personal population explosion to get her.

Mae came back with the thermos, then busied herself setting it and a fresh cup out for him.

'I brought you a couple of cookies,' she said. 'Just in case.' She didn't say in case of what.

'Thanks.' He glanced up distractedly. He was busy wondering if there was a legal limit on the number of kids you could claim for taxes.

'Mae, have you got any kids?' he asked

abruptly.

'Not yet. Someday though,' she said, eyes dreamy, voice wistful. She started stroking the thermos as if it could kick start the process.

Women. Weird. Mention babies and sometimes their brains went into meltdown. 'How many do you want?'

She turned pink, as if he'd asked her what kind of birth control she favored. 'I don't know. A couple. Kids are expensive.'

'Uh huh!' Kent slapped a hand on his desk hard enough to send a stapler thudding to the floor. 'My argument exactly. Why have a team when a pair will do, right?'

Mae shot him a confused look, and no damn wonder. He and Mae hadn't had anything remotely like a personal conversation since she'd joined Beachline.

He rubbed his forehead again, about where his dunce cap should sit. 'Forget it. Thanks for the coffee.' He reached for his cup and opened a file, hoping she'd take the hint and leave. She did.

With Mae gone, Kent leaned back in his chair, nursing his coffee as if it were hundred-year-old Scotch. He was losing it. Completely losing it. If he didn't get a grip on this thing he had for O'Hanlon, someone was going to put him in a rubber room. He let out breath enough to drain his lungs. Trouble was he didn't want to get a grip on anything but Rosie. All of Rosie. But he didn't want to do it under

114

false pretenses.

But there was nothing he could do about it now. Rosie had faxed him saying she was going back to Borneo until Saturday. He hadn't even bothered to call. No point. Like it or not, his sanity and his hyperactive libido would have to wait, which was probably just as well. He had enough on his plate, not to mention a lousy dinner meeting on Friday with Packard. The guy hadn't taken no for an answer. Said he had some new ideas for the new wing. Kent figured it was more like some new ideas for increasing the costs, but because he didn't have anything better to do, he'd agreed to the dinner.

He checked his calendar. Friday at seven-thirty. Monk's.

In the meantime, he'd be busy enough to keep his mind off Rosie. At least he had the advantage of the barbecue, which made him her first post brace date. Maybe it was a small edge, and maybe Rosie didn't know it was a date, but for want of anything better, he'd take it.

Come Saturday he'd begin his campaign in earnest.

*   *   *

Rosie hopped her way to the kitchen telephone, struggling to plug her heel into her sneaker. Shoe in one hand, phone in the other, she sank into the fireside wing chair and

115

managed a breathless, 'Hello.'

'She lives.'

'Hey, Jonesy.' Rosie dropped the sneaker and wiggled her foot into it. 'What's happening?'

'My question exactly. What time do you want me to pick you up?'

'As close to three as you can make it. And puhleeze, puhleeze, don't be late. I feel like an inmate on freedom day. I can't believe I'm being unwired today.'

'Want to celebrate?'

'Absolutely. Have you got a plan?' With her sneakers under control, Rosie slumped back in the chair and started in on her jeans' zipper.

'Better than a plan. I've got us dates, including a real live person of the masculine persuasion who's dying to meet you, *and* I've got reservations at Monk's for seven.'

Rosie stopped zipping mid belly. 'I don't know, Jonesy.'

'What don't you know?'

'I might be tired or something.'

'This from the woman who's about to embark on an intensive, well-oiled, totally focused manhunt. Or should I say daddy hunt? I don't think so.'

'I shouldn't have told you.' Rosie groused. 'Once you hear the word goal, you're unstoppable.'

'Yeah, ain't it great?' Jonesy laughed. 'So forget the delaying action. This guy is a real possibility, hunky, wealthy, and lonely, and a perfect candidate for you to kick off your campaign. Unless, of course, you've changed your mind and want to go after sexy Summerton? Like any sane woman would.'

'No, I haven't changed my mind.' Now all she had to do is get him out of it. Saturday. She'd find his blessed Gardenia and get out of his career path.

'So, are you in or out for tonight?'

Rosie tugged at her hair in a desperate attempt to locate the enthusiasm sector of her brain. No go. This was definitely an oh-why-not decision rather than the yes!—let's-do-it kind. Irritating. And all because of a pair of green eyes to die for.

And something was poking into her backside.

'Rosie?'

She reached under her behind and pulled out her glasses. Broken. Again. Of course it was Summerton's fault. Everything was Summerton's fault. Ever since he'd knocked on her door and tantalized her with that aphrodisiac aftershave he insisted he didn't wear, she'd been completely off kilter. Well, no more. He wasn't right for her. She wasn't right for him. That was the truth of the matter. It was time she thought of her kids, and past time for Summerton and his workaholic righteousness to get out of her life. She blew out a breath strong enough to tilt a windmill.

'I'm in,' she said, then started searching her hair for a paper clip to repair her glasses. The damn things were never in the right place at the right time.

'Great,' Jonesy said. 'See you around three. I'd suggest we go shopping before we meet the guys, but knowing the current state of your finances, that would be irresponsible of me. So I'll drive you home after your doctor's appointment and pick you up again at six-thirty. I know you'll be driving again, but we might as well stick with one car. If Roland works out—'

'Who's Roland?'

'Your date, idiot.'

'Oh, yeah. Right.'

'If *Roland* works out,' Jonesy repeated, enunciating carefully, 'He can drive you home. If not, give me a high sign, and I'll do the honors. Okay?'

'Okay.'

'And Rosaleen?'

'Uh-huh?'

'Try to curb your enthusiasm. You don't want to overwhelm the guy on the first date.'

Rosie hung up the phone and went in search of a clip to fix her glasses. Roland? Were there actually men called Roland?

* * *

Kent tilted his head, then cupped his ear in an

effort to hear whatever it was Vince Packard said. Something about following him. He nodded, and they walked a gauntlet of full tables, dropping apologies as they went. It was impossible to make headway without bumping into one chair or another at every turn.

Monk's was Friday night jammed, and as noisy as a jet-test center. Hardly the place to discuss business. Kent looked around, eyes narrowing—unless it was monkey business. This place was definitely a singles hangout. He hated places like this. He hoped this wasn't an effort on Packard's part for some male bonding of the pick-up-chicks-and-party variety. If it was, he'd made a strategic error.

After they'd shouldered their way through the crowd, taken their seats, and ordered predinner drinks, Packard left to make a phone call. The waiter brought the drinks, and Kent nursed his, trying to figure out a way to cut this evening short and get back to Beachline. He had work to do. Most of which was Con's. He should damn well leave it for him. Do him good.

Kent imagined Con returning to Beachline from Hawaii and finding a stack of files on his desk high enough to obscure the view of the first tee. Every time he thought about Con his gut clenched, a knotted blend of anger and regret. Anger about the work Con didn't do, sure, but he also missed how it used to be when they'd bought the place. They'd worked together then, side-by-side in a effective partnership, and it had been great. Much as he hated to admit it, he missed the guy.

Kent made idle circles on the table top with his glass. Maybe when he came back, he'd talk to him, try to work things out. Or buy him out. He closed his eyes briefly. The thought of handling Beachline alone gave him pause. Which made no sense at all, because that's exactly what he'd been doing for months. But he had no desire to make it a permanent condition. He took a swallow of Scotch, shoved Con out of his mind, and leaned back in his chair.

He had pleasanter things to think about, like a certain quirky, one-of-a-kind woman with the maternal instinct of a rabbit, who, in a matter of days, had so turned him on that his wake-up condition was painfully predictable. Waking up aroused was okay when a man could do something about it, but when his only something was an icy shower, he was in a bad way. Yeah, if it was just good old-fashioned lust, he'd have alternatives. He glanced disinterestedly around the packed room. More than one opportunity in this place. He stifled a yawn.

His nose picked up on a scent. Something from the kitchen. Clove. Cinnamon. Both. He swiveled in his chair.

Rosie. She hadn't spotted him yet, even though she was only about three feet away, sitting with Jonesy. His whole body straightened, and his hand fell away from his drink. He couldn't believe he'd missed her on the way in. Maybe because she looked so . . . different. Her brace was gone, exposing a pale, delicate neck, and her hair was swept back and up in a wild head-topping arrangement that would baffle a NASA scientist. She was spectacular.

And a man's arm was draped casually on the back of her chair.

She was with someone.

A blast of unexpected jealousy effectively halted all normal thought processes in his brain. By the time it cleared, he found himself calmly evaluating two courses of rational action. Either doing the cave man thing—which involved bludgeoning her date with a steel-studded cudgel and dragging Rosie from the room by her copper hair—or heeding the sage advice of a recent deodorant commercial: 'Never let 'em see you sweat.'

Still undecided, he got to his feet. They led him directly to Rosie.

CHAPTER EIGHT

'That's nice. That's real nice,' Rosie said, trying to widen her eyes enough to appear somewhat interested. Not that it mattered.

Roland was a lot more interested in Roland than conversational feedback.

What the heck had Jonesy been thinking of to set her up with this guy? She looked at her watch. The way she had it figured, she'd been here about six weeks, and they hadn't even been served dinner yet. There had to be a way out of this date. She massaged her newly accessible throat and clamped her teeth over a welling yawn. Maybe she could convince ole Roland to FedEx his ego to her place. She'd stroke it a few hundred times and send it back. Easier for all concerned. While Roland droned on about Roland, she tried to come up with an escape plan.

She couldn't risk kicking Jonesy under the table again, or the woman would be going home in a wheelchair. Obviously Jonesy liked her own date. Sheesh!

Should've brought my own car, darn it. If Jonesy reneges on her promise to drive me home, I'll—

'What are you doing here, O'Hanlon?'

The voice came from behind her, cool and unfriendly. Rosie looked up and into the last pair of eyes she expected to see. And of course she was immediately warm all over, glad, mad, and befuddled.

'Kent?' she questioned, hitting a high note on the dumb response-meter.

'Last I checked,' he said mirthlessly, nodding in Jonesy's direction and giving her a smile that looked as though it had already been used. Jonesy raised a brow and grinned back. Without acknowledging the two men at the table, Kent turned his gaze back to Rosie and positively glowered at her.

'Shouldn't you be home in bed?' He gestured toward her naked neck and glared.

She stared, certain she looked like an owl on Prozac. Kent hadn't so much as glanced at Roland, and Rosie knew she should be angry at his high-handedness, his surly tone, and his lack of good manners, but she was either too stupidly pleased that he'd shown up or too leaden with boredom to drum up the necessary fire. She'd figure out which later. A golden opportunity knocked.

She reached down, gripped her bag as if it were a life preserver, and stood. 'You're absolutely right. That's precisely where I should be. And you're the perfect man to take me there.' She shot a quick glance at Roland, who was blinking so fast he couldn't work his mouth. 'You'll excuse us, won't you? Thanks so much.'

It was Kent's turn to blink. But to his credit, he didn't hesitate. He took her arm and steered her through the crowd as if he were Moses and Monk's was the Red Sea. He stopped briefly to speak to a man sitting at one of the tables, and the next minute they were outside waiting for the parking attendant to bring his car around.

Rosie breathed deep of the cool evening air. She'd been unforgivably rude, but she doubted she'd so much as scuffed Roland's sacred selfhood. She was just happy to be free and standing next to the man she lov—.

Her knees threatened to give out. Trembling, she tried to stuff that scary thought back in the dream bag it had escaped from. Lust, she reminded herself, it was only lust. Not that there was anything 'only' about it. Not if the object of said lust occupied your thoughts every waking minute and had you consumed with curiosity about . . . all kinds of things.

Like what he'd look like naked, what his hands would feel like against your skin, if his lovemaking would be teasingly gentle or erotically rough, if he'd want the lights on or off; what his first words would be after making love . . .

She slipped off her jacket and pressed her fingers against her chest bone. Her mouth was dry.

She realized that Kent hadn't said a word since they left the restaurant.

'Kent, I—'

'Here's the car,' he said abruptly.

The attendant opened the door for her, and she slid in, seconds before Kent took his place in the driver's seat. Without a word, he peeled away from the curb.

It took a few minutes for Rosie to get

124

courage enough to try again. 'Thanks for the rescue,' she said.

'You're welcome.' He gave her a quick, hard glance, then said, 'What were you doing in that place anyway?'

'I'll be gracious and not ask you the same question—'

'Business. Strictly business.'

'Whatever you say, Summerton.'

'I said it was business. Now it's your turn.'

'I think it's obvious I had a date.'

'Some date.'

She felt no need to defend Roland. 'Yeah, it was kind of a disaster. First of many, I guess.' She cringed inwardly. She couldn't believe it. After her first night out, she'd already lost enthusiasm for her daddy hunt. She was beginning to think becoming a nun and working with kids in the Third World would be easier than finding the right man, a man who wanted what she so desperately desired. No. Needed.

Kent went quiet again, then said softly, 'Why, Rosie? Why that guy instead of me?'

Rosie's tummy tumbled. 'I think we've already talked about this, Summerton. And agreed to disagree.'

He nodded, looking weary. 'The family thing.'

He drove on in silence until they reached the turn into her driveway. He made it smoothly and pulled up in front of her stairs.

Rosie couldn't make herself get out of the car. Lady Brain was AWOL, leaving Hormone to conjure and imagine . . .

What would he taste like? Feel like pressed into her body in the moonlight? Would he whisper in her ear when he came? Would he smile and kiss her throat when they'd both had enough? Could there ever be enough?

Kent neither moved nor spoke. He rested his hand along the back of the seat and played with her hair. He appeared thoughtful, speculative.

'Rosie, what if I changed my mind? What if I said I'd consider making your dream mine?'

Her heart lifted, then skittered, then fell. 'You'd give up your ninety hour work week and computer scheduler to make time for me and a row of runny-nosed kids? I don't think so.'

He stroked her neck, and she let him, shifting so she could feel his fingers glide along her hair line. Her skin was maddeningly sensitive there and dangerously susceptible to his touch. She leaned against his hand, capturing it between her shoulder and chin. 'You should stop.'

He didn't stop, but pulled his hand free and moved it to the other side of her neck.

'Why wouldn't it work?' he asked quietly.

She tried to concentrate, to ignore the play of his fingers on her skin. 'Because you'd be saying it to get me into bed, and you'd change your mind later. After you got what you wanted.'

His hand stopped, then started again. 'What we both want, Red.'

She felt him tug her closer, didn't try to resist. When he drew her face to his, questioned her with his eyes, she nodded. 'What we both want.'

He kissed her—so completely she was filled with it. And as her universe shrank to encompass only the blissful space filled by their bodies, the hot link of their mouths, she knew she was perilously near to letting Hormone rule and possibly making the biggest mistake of her life.

She wasn't completely sure, but she was pretty sure she was about to have sex with Kent Summerton.

She refused to call it making love. No point to that. Love was forever. Love included the kids she wanted to have, and a man who'd be a husband and dad first, and a business tycoon second. Kent Summerton was a classic workaholic with scarcely enough time to eat, let alone nurture a dozen kids. Well, maybe a dozen was a *bit* much.

'Are you going to invite me in?' he murmured against her throat, his breath warm enough to melt a steel chastity belt. Rosie was sure she heard Hormone's garters snap. Kent nuzzled her just under the ear.

Her insides turned syrupy and warm.

Lady Brain, come in please. Mayday. Mayday.

He kissed her neck, effectively sabotaging all communication. His low voice with its implied wonders tugged at her heartstrings—along with a few other strings attached to more sinful parts of her female anatomy.

Oh, hell. Why couldn't things ever be easy. *Invite him in . . .* His question was definitely the line in the sand. Cross it and she risked her heart. She wasn't so far into her sexual fantasy she couldn't see that. Resistance. That's what was needed here.

He ran a slow finger from her ear to her shoulder, pushing aside her stretchy top as he went. And followed it with his mouth.

On the other hand, it was a chance to test all her wild imaginings. He cupped her breast, grazed his thumb over her nipple. She closed her eyes.

'And if I do?' Her words came out on whispery, wimpy breath. She wasn't pleased with herself. She forced herself to look up at him, wanting to see what his eyes said.

'We'll just . . . talk. If that's what you want.' He grinned, as if the idea held merit as a practical joke, then sobered. 'I want you, Red.' His gaze intensified, darkened. 'And I care about you. Enough to complicate your life and mine. I'm not promising anything—' he traced an imaginary line across the swell of her breasts '—except a good time, but I'd like you to give us a chance.'

128

A chance. Could there be one? She doubted it, but the idea made her heart leap like a crazed dolphin. She was hopeless. Utterly hopeless. And she was too turned on to care. If this was a mistake, it wouldn't be her first one. But the rock-bottom truth was, if she didn't make love with this man, she'd regret it the rest of her life.

'Rosie,' he said, lightly kissing her ear. 'I really do like kids.'

She laughed, pulled away, and touched his cheek. 'You're shameless, Summerton. Completely shameless. But liking kids isn't enough to get you into my bed.'

'Damn. I figured that was my best shot.' He smiled and raised a brow. 'So what *will* get me into your bed?'

Rosie took a long, steadying breath and sent Lady Brain for pizza. 'Actually, I'm kind of intrigued by that good time you promised.'

*　　　*　　　*

They stood facing each other in Rosie's bedroom, an indoor garden of color caught in the day's last light. Pinks, greens, and brushstrokes of yellow blended to a gay and inviting harmony. A brass bed sat near an open window, its metal sending glittery winks into the room with each rise of the breeze-tossed curtains.

They held hands, and Kent leaned down to

kiss Rosie's forehead. It was a soft kiss, cool and gentle, before he freed his hands from hers and gripped her shoulders, pulling her close.

Her insides quivered, half in anticipation and half in horrendous nervousness. It had been a while since she'd done this. A long while. And because it was nothing like riding a bicycle, she was pretty sure a person forgot how. Not that she had much to remember. There been a few gropes and fumbles along the way, but mostly she'd messed them up. She expected a complete botch-up on her part, a nightmare of adolescent awkwardness, yanked hair, and teeth collisions.

'Thank you, O'Hanlon,' Kent said somewhere close to her ear.

'What for? We haven't done anything yet.' She rested her head against his heart, listened to its beat. Strong, but none too steady. She took satisfaction in that.

'I know. I just wanted you to know it means something to me. Being here. In your room.'

'Oh, well then, you're welcome. I guess.'

'You're nervous.'

'No, I—' Her head came up, clipped him hard on the chin. You could have heard his teeth rattle from the kitchen. 'I'm sorry. God, I'm sorry.' She knew she'd blow it. She just knew it. Sharon Stone, she wasn't.

'You *are* nervous.'

She stepped back, the better to look him in

the eyes—and avoid inflicting further wounds. She was pretty sure he'd function better if he hit the bed in one piece. 'You're right, Summerton, I am. I'm a bedroom klutz. Think of your worst nightmare of a sex partner; gauche, bumbling, inept and I'm it. And—' Lord almighty, she was going to cry '—and I don't want to be that way with you. The truth is I'm a big mouth with more sass than brass. If you know what I mean.'

With reckless disregard for his own safety, he pulled her to him. 'O'Hanlon, you're something. Really something.' He ran his hands along her shoulders, up her neck and past her ears to sink his hands deep in her hair. 'Why not relax and leave it to me? I'm the one who promised the good time.'

'True.' She wrapped her arms around his waist and hung on. She sniffed. 'Okay, how about I pretend I'm one of those inflatable doll things and leave you to it.'

He leaned back and laughed, and his laughter soothed like a cool compress on a nasty fever. She giggled against his chest.

Still laughing, he picked her up as easily as though she were made of gossamer and cobwebs, and carried her to the bed. But when he stood over her and started to undo the buttons on his shirt, and she caught her first glimpse of his satiny chest hair, she sat up immediately. Her fervid imaginings were about to become reality, and she didn't want to miss a thing.

'Hey, this is a two way street, you know.'

He might have been complaining, but, thankfully, he didn't stop—until he was down to his slacks and an undone zipper. Rosie couldn't take her eyes off that strip of metal. He flicked open the button on his slacks and arched a brow. 'Rosie?'

She lifted her arms high above her head. 'I'm a rubber doll, remember?' The idea of letting him do all the work was more appealing by the minute.

No hesitation and no awkwardness, he just pulled her cotton tee over her head and joined her on the bed. Then he hooked his fingers under the spaghetti straps of her bra and dropped them over her shoulders. 'Turn around,' he instructed.

She turned, lifted her hair, and he undid her bra. The instant it fell away, he replaced it with his hands, lifting her breasts as if savoring the weight of them. He kissed her back, played his thumbs over her already hardened nipples. 'Perfect,' he murmured between kisses. He cupped her again. 'Exactly right.'

Rosie couldn't breathe. Her vision blurred. Okay, this would be a first. She was going to faint before the good part. 'Kent, I think you'd better stop doing that,' she mumbled.

Thank heavens he didn't hear her.

He caught her nipple gently between two fingers and rolled it. Using his other hand to lift her hair away from her neck, he kissed her nape and shoulders, a hundred nipping kisses that made her body as soft as summer butter.

She was definitely going to faint.

Kent stopped, rested his head on her shoulder, and groaned softly against her skin. His hands idled below her breasts. 'Rosie?'

'Hm-m?'

'Your neck. Is it okay? I mean *really* okay? I don't want to hurt you in any way.'

Hurt? All she could think about was pleasure and those lazy, mind-bending semicircles he'd started making under the point of her breast with his thumb. She put a hand over his. Sucked in some air. 'Headstands are out. That's about it.'

'Good, but I'll be careful anyway.' He gave her one more kiss on the neck, turned her to face him, and cradled her until she was stretched out on the bed beneath him. Supporting himself on one elbow, he stared at her, eyes glittering and dark. A hank of his rich brown hair fell forward and Rosie reached for it, stroked it back. Thick and lively, it resisted her attempt to contain it, and she was glad because she loved the feel of it gliding over her palms, slipping through her fingers.

Kent ran a lazy finger down the cleft between her breasts, flattened his hand, and slid it under her skirt waistband and across her belly. Everywhere he touched she warmed. His movements were languid and easy, as if he had all the time in the world. He started on the long line of buttons on the front of her skirt, easing them open with one hand while leaning to kiss her breast, play on it with his tongue. Nerves tingled, muscles pulled and relaxed. Rosie gave way to it, sinking deeper into the soft mattress.

'That feels good,' she heard herself murmur. Eyes closing, she lifted her upper torso to his lips. She knew what she wanted, but couldn't say it. Didn't have to. Kent took her nipple fully into his mouth and suckled, pulling hard, pulling her deep.

Rosie's mind numbed. She couldn't still herself, couldn't stop the clamoring of her body, the soft rush of moist heat.

Never.

She'd never felt like this before. She'd scream when he touched her where she so wanted to be touched. But if he didn't touch her there, and soon, she'd scream even louder. God, she was going to shriek and burst his eardrum. She clamped her mouth shut.

'Lift your hips, Red.'

She lifted them, and he pulled her skirt from under her, disposed of her panties, then his slacks. The man was good. And highly aroused. He rested his hand on the inside of her knee, and she watched his gaze travel slowly over every bit of her exposed skin, pausing at her breasts, stopping at the vee between her legs. His gaze met hers the moment his hand cupped her. And while she struggled for breath, Kent's eyes narrowed, clouded with erotic intimacy.

He kissed her ear, his hand moving over and through her heat. 'I knew you'd be special,' he whispered roughly. 'I love your skin.' He ran his hand down the inside of her thigh, then up again, finally back to where she wanted it, this time fingering her deeply. She gasped and arched into his hand. 'Like satin. Beautiful.' He returned to her breast, the strong tug of his mouth in perfect unity with his roving, stroking fingers.

She moved to his hand, in a questing undulation she couldn't control and didn't want to. She wanted to purr, but she moaned instead, her breath tangling in her throat as he went deeper still.

Rosie wanted to touch him, wanted to feel him strong and heavy in her hand, but he stopped her.

'Later, love,' he said in a strangled voice, pulling away from her briefly. Before she could open her eyes to see what was he doing, he was back. With one easy, fluid move, he covered her, nudged her thighs apart, and rested himself against her. His erection was a brand; long, hard, and sinfully hot.

Every gene, fiber, and nerve in Rosie's body anticipated him, longed for him.

He poised over her, probed gently for entry—and sank deep. His plunge, smooth and faultless, filled her to her core.

Dazed with sensation, Rosie met his strong, powerful thrusts, again and again, inwardly pleading for more. She scraped her nails along his back, dug them into his muscled shoulders. And she bit her lips, sealed them tight.

'Don't,' Kent said in a strained voice; kissing her hard. 'Let it come. Let me know how you feel.'

'I feel like . . . like I'm breaking up.'

When he gripped her buttocks and lifted her to him, held her firm to thrust deeper, she gasped and sunk her nails into his biceps. 'No. Yes. No more. Oh, yes. I can't—'

'Let it happen, Red. Let go.'

He shifted slightly, so the whole hard length of him, rubbed hotly against her—in her. Her body pulsed and writhed as she grabbed fistfuls of the sheet for anchor.

He held himself above her, almost but not quite out. Only air against her breasts—where Kent should have been.

She heard her ragged moan fill the darkening room, felt the rumble of a heart beating so wildly it threatened to leap from her chest. She wanted, ached with need, but there couldn't be more. She couldn't take any more. She opened her eyes, and they met Kent's, black and hot with sex and erotic challenge.

'Come to me, Red,' he demanded.

Gazes locked, she gripped his straining biceps and lifted her body to his, invited him.

He lowered himself, his hair tangling with hers, and came back to her, going deeper, holding, going deeper yet, taking her exactly where she wanted to go—with him.

CHAPTER NINE

Kent's body thundered to a state of collapse. He felt like shouting for joy, but he was too exhausted. Spent and empty from the kind of lovemaking a man only dreams about.

He hoped Rosie felt the same.

He rolled off her and tugged her to a warm spot under his arm, kissing her hair, the lingering heat on her forehead. He could hold her all night. Or do a lot more than hold. The night had barely begun.

She sat up abruptly, jabbing an elbow into his chest to gain leverage. Her eyes were moon-wide. 'We didn't use anything!'

He disengaged from her elbow, rubbed where he was sure to bruise, and swung his feet to the floor on the other side of the bed. He looked back at her. 'Is that right?'

'What if I'm pregnant?' She skittered up the bed and pulled the quilt up like a shield, presumably against marauding sperm.

'Given your goal in life, I'd think that would make you a happy woman.'

She gave him a scathing look, and he

grinned. Jonesy was right, Rosie did have a problem with priorities. Most women would have thought of protection before, rather than after. Not that he'd given her much chance. He ambled into the bathroom. When he came back, she was staring out the window, looking fretful and adorable.

His stomach knotted, and he sensed a definite unbalancing of sorts in the vicinity of his chest. Love? Odd. The thought didn't bother him in the least. But the idea of the statistic-popping family Rosie wanted scared him half to death. He hoped she'd start thinking more rationally after tomorrow, because he wanted a lot more than good-time sex with this woman. A lot more.

'It's okay. I used something,' he said.

Her gaze swung round. 'You did not.'

'Yes, I did.'

'Didn't.'

He grinned. 'Did so.'

She frowned, as if trying to remember, and pulled the blanket higher.

'Rosie, I would not lie about something like that.' He stooped and picked up the empty foil packet from beside the bed, handed it to her. 'Satisfied?'

She looked puzzled. 'When did you put a condom on? I didn't notice . . .'

He sat on the edge of the bed, and touched her crazy hair. 'That's because you were blind with passion.'

'I was not.'

'Were so.'

'Was—' She stopped, then smiled. 'Okay, Summerton, you're right. I have to admit the rubber doll thing really worked for me,' she added dryly.

'Glad to hear it. Maybe I'll give it a try.'

'Maybe you should,' she said, then tugged him to the bed, and drew his face to hers, kissing him with more exuberance than passion. 'I loved it!'

It was his turn to frown. 'The rubber doll thing?' He was definitely having trouble following this conversation.

'No, you idiot. What we did together. The sex. I loved it. And you know what? I've never really loved sex before. I've always wondered what all the fuss was about.' She kissed him again, looking righteously pleased with herself. 'And now I know.'

A weird warmth filled his lungs. He didn't know what to say, so he said nothing, just stretched out beside her and tucked her in close. When she leaned over to kiss him, and her hair clouded across his chest, he stroked her head, then lifted her chin so he could look into her eyes.

'What I said, about you being special, Rosie, I meant. I'd like—'

She shushed him and touched his lips with two fingers. 'Don't! If we talk, my imaginary kids will get in the way. For tonight, let's just pretend they're all tucked safely in their beds, and we're an old married couple with the door locked.' She kissed him and nibbled on his lower lip.

It was the most unromantic scenario he could possibly imagine, but it didn't stop him from yanking her to him and giving her a lot more kiss than she bargained for. 'If chat's how you want to play it, *old* woman, we'd better not waste any time.'

'Oh, yes, let's not.' She lifted her head. 'You do have more of those silver packets, don't you?'

'Enough,' he said, hoping it wasn't a lie.

*   *   *

At five A.M. Kent kissed Rosie's shoulder.

'I've got to go, Red,' he whispered in her ear. Her response was an inarticulate grunt. He tried a gentle tug on her hair. This time she groaned and pulled the blanket over her head. He didn't like leaving without saying goodbye. It didn't feel right. He swung his feet to the floor and looked back at her. Or rather at a mass of red hair that fringed the blanket covering her face. Much as he wanted to see her open her eyes, dousing her with ice water was out of the question. He pulled the blanket down, kissed her shoulder again, then stood.

It took all his willpower to walk away from her bed, but he didn't have a choice. It would

140

be light soon, and he had work to do before the family barbecue. Work. There was never a shortage of that. And for the first time the idea ticked him off.

After showering, he walked back into the bedroom, hoping to find Rosie awake. But she was still snuggled into sleep. He stood quietly, toweling himself off, unable to take his eyes off her. He swore. He was hard again. This from a guy who just weeks ago figured he was in sexual decline. But then he hadn't met Rosie.

He wanted her.

He loved her.

Thank God for Gardenia was his next thought. Whoever she was—and he didn't really care anymore—he owed her. If not for her, he'd never have met his Rosie.

Yeah, he loved her, and he intended to do something about it. And his plans didn't include her going to a singles dance tonight. Or a baseball team of kids. He wrapped the towel around his shoulders and headed back to the bathroom.

'You've got great buns, Summerton.'

He turned to face her, and she looked brazenly at his erection. He felt a surge of blood, a binding of muscle, and was surprised to find he was mildly embarrassed.

Her eyes lifted to his. 'You weren't planning on wasting that, were you?'

He headed to the bed, sat on its edge, and twisted to lean over her. 'I had some ideas, if

I'd been able to raise the dead.' He kissed her nipple, breathed in the scent of sex and cinnamon emanating from her warm skin. It hit him like a power surge.

But he damn well didn't have time. When he pulled back she wrapped her arms around him and buried her face in his shoulder.

'You know what I said last night, about never having enjoyed sex until you?' She paused. 'It was true.'

'I'm glad.' That was the understatement of the year.

'Now I've got another confession to make.'

'Uh-huh?' he kissed her head, ran a hand down her back. He really did have to go. Had to.

'I've never made love in the morning. It's just . . . never happened.'

She reached down and took his hardness in her hand, circled him like a velvet vise. He restrained a gasp, but couldn't stop his eyes from closing, couldn't stop his mind from centering on the pressure of her hand.

To hell with work. 'Until now, Rosie. Until now.'

*   *   *

'Isn't it amazing? The weather is perfect. You know, I don't think we've had a bad day in the ten years we've been having these barbecues,' his mother said.

Kent nodded, and for the hundredth time looked at the French doors leading to the Beachline patio where he and his mother sat under a large tent.

He wished he hadn't let Rosie insist on driving herself today. What if she went straight through to the accounting office? He might miss her entirely. He tried not to think what her reaction would be when she realized the barbecue she'd refused to attend with him was today. His only hope was that last night had changed things between them, and she'd cut him some slack. He looked back at the doors.

'What time is it?' he asked, taking a drink from his coffee and ignoring the silver and gold watch on his wrist.

'Quarter to twelve,' his mother said, then excitedly raised her hand. 'Oh, look, here come John and Nancy. Don't they look wonderful? The move to Bothell obviously agrees with them.'

'Where in hell is Bothell? And when did they move there?'

His mother gave him one of her get-a-grip looks, then sighed, one of those long-suffering, mother-type sighs. 'Really, Kent, you could at least keep track of where your cousins live.'

Before he could defend himself by telling her he'd need to hire a full-time staffer if he even tried to account for all his relatives' whereabouts, she was waving wildly at some new arrivals; his brother, Mike, his wife,

Leona, and their two-and-a half-year-old twin girls, Emma and Jane. His nieces, he reminded himself, thinking it had been a long time since he seen them. They'd grown. Looking at their beaming faces, he warmed inside. With those smiles, their bright summer dresses and straw hats, they were real little heartbreakers.

'Unken Ken. We're here,' they said in excited harmony. They were beautiful, and he found he didn't mind a bit when they ran up to him and planted kisses on his cheeks. But then, they weren't sticky yet. Give 'em time, he thought. He watched them run off to play with their zillion cousins, then bear-hugged his brother and kissed Leona. He didn't know how they did it. Or why. Mike and Leona had three boys already in school when the twins came along. Kent knew Leona's pregnancy was no accident. He and Mike were alike that way, both into planning and controlling everything they could, both ambitious. But they sure as hell parted company when it came to the family thing.

'So, who's the woman?' Mike asked, the split second Leona and his mother left to start harassing Beachline's professional catering staff.

Kent's gaze shot to Mike's grinning face. 'What woman?' He decided to play dumb. He wasn't quite ready for the family's inevitable scrutiny of every hair on Rosie's Technicolor head.

Mike patted him on the back, gave him a knowing look. 'It's okay. We've all been there. Mom had me married to Leona from our first date—which, by the way, was a disaster. Why should you be exempt from her predictions?'

'Maybe because I haven't even got to the first-date stage yet.' Kent was surprised to realize what he said was true. He and Rosie hadn't dated in the traditional dinner-and-candlelight sense. They'd kind of blasted past the preliminaries and gone straight to dessert. He remembered this morning and his groin tightened.

'It doesn't matter.' Mike swept a hand to encompass the patio and garden area, already awash in Summertons and assorted in-laws. 'We've all been put on notice to be on our best behavior. Which means, I presume, no drooling in our soup, because what's between you and this mystery lady is, according to Mom, "*very* serious".'

'She said that?' Kent was dumbstruck. He'd barely mentioned Rosie.

'Uh-huh, that she did.' Mike clapped him on the shoulder, and gave him a broadly sympathetic look. 'And from what I'm told, if you don't nab this one, bro, you're headed for a state of permanent bachelorhood.'

'I can think of worse things.'

Mike's gaze shifted to where his wife was standing beside his mother, one hand on Jane's golden head, the other on Emma's. 'I can't,' he said quietly, then turned back to beam at Kent, again gesturing with his hand to indicate the growing crowd. 'Hope she knows what she's in for.'

Kent's gaze followed Mike's hand just in time to see his sister Jayne's boy, Zach, stumble, break a glass, knock over a plant, rip his pants, and smear vanilla ice cream on his Uncle Joe's black slacks in one non-stop motion.

'Not a clue.' He grinned at the Zach debacle. 'But she will before the day's over.'

*   *   *

Rosie pulled her Geo into the last parking spot in the lot. She glanced around. Whatever was going on at Beachline must be big. The place was jammed. She grabbed her tote and eased herself out of the car. She was the tiniest bit sore, enough to remind her of the night before and the early morning hours she'd spent with Kent. She guessed that's what happened when you'd been out of the mating game as long as she had. Well, she'd come back with a vengeance last night. She tried not to grin, and wondered if her satisfaction would show on her face like a trowel load of too much makeup. She swung her bag over her shoulder and headed across the parking lot for Beachline's glass and brass front doors.

Mating game.

The words made her spirits droop like week-old tulips. The singles dance thing was tonight. She didn't want to attend. She wanted to go back to bed with Kent. But that wasn't going to happen. She and Lady Brain had agreed on that this morning. One hot night did not a family man make. Kent Summerton was no more marriage material this morning—or less work obsessed—than he had been yesterday. Less, in her mind.

She hadn't missed that his whispered allusions to 'a chance for them,' and his lust-filled offer to 'make her dream his,' were conspicuously absent after lovemaking. She'd forgotten. She called it lovemaking. He simply called it sex.

Okay, she wasn't surprised, but it did hurt. Which was, as usual, her own darn fault.

Rosie O'Hanlon had always been too quick to believe, to trust, to go with the flow. Until now. She knew what she wanted, and she intended to get it. An old-fashioned guy who'd put family time before overtime. And she would not waste her ovaries' productive years converting a man from scheduler worship to baby love. If he refused to see it was more worthwhile to produce good kids than a balanced budget, so be it.

Rosie swung open the doors of Beachline with gusto and headed straight for accounting. She was on a mission. She would make sure she heard every voice in the place today, identify Gardenia, and head back to Borneo.

What was wrong with the world anyway? she groused to herself, striding down the hall. What was so crazy about wanting to have more than the statistically-correct number of kids and be a dedicated, full-time mom? Maybe she was out of step with the times, but she couldn't be the only one. There must be a man out there somewhere who wanted what she wanted. Believed what she believed, that nothing—absolutely nothing—came before family. Kids mattered, damn it. They mattered more than anything! Why couldn't Summerton see that? She'd pegged him right from the get-go. Nothing but a suit in hunk's clothing. Sheesh! She gave the door to accounting a major thwack and marched in. Or was about to.

'Rosie.' It was Kent.

She stopped mid-doorway and nearly choked on her own breath. The last time she'd seen Kent, about five hours ago, he was naked as sin, and so was she. They were in her shower and she'd dropped the shampoo bottle on his toe. When she got on her knees to retrieve it, she'd . . . well, she'd got kind of carried away, and done something she'd never done before. Not that Kent had complained . . .

Praying for a potent shot of post-coital sophistication, she turned. Obviously God was busy giving some football player another touchdown, because her face immediately heated to a full boil. Her tote caught on the door handle, and the strap broke, spilling pens, combs, brushes, Juicy Fruit gum, and miscellaneous feminine hygiene products onto the lushly carpeted hall.

Kent's polished shoe crushed a tampon.

He bent down, picked it up, and handed it to her as if it were a buck and she a street urchin.

She knew her face couldn't get any redder, so she just mumbled, 'Thanks,' and stuffed it in her one-strap bag. She wanted to stuff her head in there too, but she forced her chin up and looked at him.

'You came,' he said, looking entirely too pleased with himself. He reached out a hand.

Certain he was going to touch her hair, she stepped back. 'Gardenia, remember? Today's the day. I thought I'd start in accounting because that's where I spent the most time when I was here last.'

He dropped his hand. 'Good idea. But you must be hungry. How about lunch first? It's a beautiful day. We can eat on the patio. You can do some listening and eat at the same time.'

'I don't feel like eating.' *Unless it's you.* Oh, lord, Hormone was back. Rosie was in trouble.

'Well, I do, and I have something I want you to see.' He offered his hand again. When she ignored it, he stepped up beside her and

149

leaned to talk quietly in her ear. 'Last night, you were nervous. Today, you're embarrassed.' He kissed her ear so lightly she thought she imagined it. 'Believe me, Red, you have nothing to be embarrassed about. You were magnificent.' He tugged on her elbow.

Rosie went along. A girl had to eat.

CHAPTER TEN

The no-good, low-down sneak.

Rosie stopped in her tracks and took a good look around to be absolutely sure. She felt his hand on the small of her back, but refused to be prodded forward.

The patio, warmed by sunshine and shaded by forest green canvas, overflowed with people and everybody was talking to somebody. Above the conversation, laughter poked the air like careless punctuation.

'This is your family barbecue,' she announced, as if the arrogant so-and-so didn't know it. Then it hit her. She scanned the happy crowd. So many people.

'This is your family barbecue?' she repeated, slightly awed. 'There must be over a hundred people here.'

'Yes, it is, and yes, there are.' His lips curved, but he had the grace—or brains—not to look too sure of himself.

'I think I'm mad. Or should be. Didn't I tell you I wouldn't come?'

'You did, but I wanted you to meet them.'

'All of them?' She swallowed. So much family. Nobody had this much family. She couldn't take her eyes off them.

'As many as you can take.' He dipped his chin, lifted hers. 'Are you really mad?'

'Yes. No. I don't know. You never told me you had a family big enough to fund their own dental plan.'

'You never asked.'

He was right. She hadn't. She'd assumed he'd been seeded in a test tube and raised in the nearest faculty of business. She had a way of assuming things. She took another look around and spotted a small dark-haired boy sticking his fingers into a large bowl of red gelatin. Kent's gaze followed hers.

'That's Zach,' Kent said. 'One of my sister's kids.'

'How many do you have? Brothers and sisters, I mean?' She was openmouthed with curiosity.

'Four brothers; Mike, Paul, Joe, and Ben, and five sisters; Marianne, Willa, Jayne, Tina, and Anne Marie.'

'Wow.' She was stunned and awed. There had always only been her mom and herself. She couldn't imagine growing up in a family like Kent's. But, oh, how she'd have loved it. Her soul glowed at the thought.

'Yeah. Wow.' Ken said, his expression bland. 'And now they all have kids of their own. Lots and lots of kids.'

At that moment, Kent was ambushed by two identical little girls who bounded up and wrapped their arms around his legs. From this vantage point, they both smiled impishly at Rosie. Kent swung one of them up and into his arms. 'This is . . . Emma?' he guessed, tilting hits head theatrically as if to get a good look

'No, Unken Ken.' She giggled and punched his shoulder. 'Mine Jane.'

'I knew that.'

'No?' She punched him again.

'Up, too. Lift me,' the other girl, who Rosie assumed must be Emma, begged. 'Peese.'

Rosie squatted down and smiled at the girl. 'Uncle Kent's got his hands full right now. How about if I lift you?'

Emma tightened her grip on Kent's leg and assessed the new person who'd just entered her fledgling universe. Rosie wondered what judgments she was making.

'I'll take you over there—' she bribed shamelessly, pointing to the red gelatin '—and you can stick your finger in the Jell-O.'

'Zach do?' Emma's eyes saucered.

'Uh-huh, except we'll get our very own bowl for our very own fingers.' She offered her hand, and when Emma grasped it in her small one, the warm balloon in Rosie's heart came near to bursting. She looked up to see Kent smiling at her, Jane's arms so tight around his neck she wondered how he drew breath.

He ruffled Jane's wispy hair, and offered Rosie his hand. As the four of them made their way to the red Jell-O, Rosie let hope take root. Kent had snookered her into being here today, so he had to have had his reasons. Maybe there was a chance for them, and maybe this was his way of telling her that. Or maybe, as usual, she was putting wishes where her priorities should be.

*   *   *

Nine o'clock. Kent took up a position at the entrance. The family was in the process of leaving. The path to the parking lot looked like an evacuation march, and the Beachline staff had the wan smiles and lethargic gestures of hurricane survivors. As for the forty-odd kids, a quarter of them were taking the over-tired whine to new heights on the sound meter, a quarter of them were sleeping in the arms of their weary parents, while the last half was equally divided between the demanding 'can-we-go-nows?' and the protesting 'don't-want to-gos!' With everyone saying good-bye at once, there was nothing to do but smile and shake hands.

Kent was tired to the bone. Not to mention frustrated and disappointed.

He'd lost connection with Rosie within

fifteen minutes of the Jell-O bowl adventure, and hadn't managed to get within fifteen feet of her since. The day hadn't gone as he'd planned.

The idea was to make sure Rosie had a clear picture of the trials and difficulties of raising a big family. He'd planned to steer her toward the day's hot spots. Like Zach's collision with the punch table. That was a beaut. Kent grinned in spite of himself. One good yank on the linen tablecloth and that punch was airborne. Zach had swiftly consigned cut glass bowl, cups, and about a hundred or so dessert plates to plastic-bag ignominy and the kitchen glassware budget to a pond of red ink.

Rosie was nowhere to be found at the time.

She'd also missed Corey spewing chocolate milk onto the front of Jane and Emma's 'very best' dresses in his attempt to make brown bubbles.

They'd been changed and had stopped wailing by the time Rosie got back from the putting green with Paul's three teenagers.

If he were a suspicious man he'd be thinking conspiracy, any of the fates, or his mother. Every time he got within talking distance of Rosie, she—or Jayne—had spirited her away, as if on cue.

He felt the warm pressure of a kiss on his cheek. His mother. 'I've got to hurry, dear, your father's already in the car. I just wanted to say thank you. The day was wonderful.' She hugged him hard. 'And just think, considering the size of the family, it will be *forever* before it's your turn to host again.'

'It was fun,' he said.

She lifted a brow that said, *'Don't kid a kidder, kid.'*

'I mean it.' And he did, which surprised him, because he'd been dreading the damn barbecue for weeks.

'I'm glad. We'll see you tomorrow, then, around eleven?'

'Uh-huh. If the weather holds, we'll eat on the east terrace.' While most of the extended family headed home after the barbecue, it was traditional for Kent's immediate family to meet for a quiet brunch the following morning. If you could call any meal taken with Zach and Corey quiet.

His mother turned away, then turned back, a gleam in her maternal eye. 'And Kent, I want to be the first to know about your and Rosie's marriage plans. You can't start too soon for these things.'

He opened his mouth to protest, then stopped and grinned. 'Mom, you're astounding.'

'I know.' She pecked him on the check again. 'So is Rosie, Kent. Don't you let that woman get away.'

*   *   *

Kent found 'that woman' sitting alone on the far edge of the now deserted patio. She had her arms crossed on the table and was resting her head on them.

She was crying.

Alarmed, he knelt beside her chair. He knew the day would be strenuous for her, but he hadn't expected this. 'What's wrong, sweetheart?' He caressed her tangle of hair, and, as always, was entranced by the vibrancy and life in it, the way it crinkled around his fingers, bright and springy.

Rosie lifted her head and sniffed. Her eyes were smudged brown from running mascara, and her nose was pink. 'Oh, Kent, I've never had such a day. The kids. All the kids. They were great, but . . . but—'

'It's okay. I know. It was probably too much for your first time out.' He caressed her neck. 'You must be exhausted. I'll take you home. You can get some rest, and we'll discuss the Summerton clan later.' He shoved her hair back from her forehead and kissed it softly. She smelled like fresh lime.

She sat up. 'I am tired, but Kent your family is wonderful. Your mom, Mike, Jayne . . . All of them. They made me feel so welcome. It was as if I belong—'

She stopped so abruptly he almost heard the words collide with the back of her teeth. When it looked as though she might cry again, he decided not to press.

'Come on, Red. Let's go home.'

On the way to the car, Rosie was unusually quiet. Either weary to her core, or totally shell-shocked by her exposure to the Summerton regiments, Kent figured. He hoped it was the latter.

*   *   *

Rosie was so busy thinking about the wonders of her day, it took her a while before she realized that Kent was heading in the opposite direction from her farmhouse.

'Hey, what's the plan here? I thought you were taking me home?'

'I am. My home.'

'Oh.' Rosie didn't know whether to bop him for assuming she'd go to his place, or give in to her curiosity about what kind of place the perfect Summerton lived in. It didn't take long for curiosity to win out. 'Okay,' she said. 'But absolutely no sex.' Might as well get the rules right up front. Until some facts fed that small hope lingering in her chest, she wasn't going to risk another mind-numbing sexual encounter. Her heart couldn't take the risk.

Kent laughed. 'Coffee and conversation, then.'

'Okay, but no passes. Not even one,' she stated firmly.

'Cross my heart,' he said, but she noticed he

157

didn't actually make the cross. No sense talking to the man. None at all. She gave him a stern glare and looked out her window. They were heading downtown. Please, please, don't let him live in a penthouse with plastic plants, she prayed. That would be the end, the absolute end. And spoil one of the most perfect days of her life.

Her mind went back to the Summerton barbecue, flicking through the day's images as though they were Polaroids. Zach's solemn handshake when they were introduced. Emma's exuberant good-bye kiss. Corey's bright blue eyes when he showed her the ladybug he'd found. Kent was so lucky to have them in his life. Couldn't he see that? See the immense importance of it? She thought of Jayne. She'd told Rosie that she was pregnant again, and when Rosie had asked if Kent knew he was going to be an uncle once more, Jayne had laughed. She'd said she wouldn't tell Kent until she was prepared to hear his usual lecture on family planning and financial responsibility. Rosie frowned. Kent was such a grinch.

She glanced up when they passed through a gate that led to a cluster of low-rise, luxury condos about a block from the waterfront. Posh. Just what she'd expected—but at least there was no elevator.

'This is it,' Kent said, pushing a button on the remote control clipped to the car's sun

158

visor. He pulled into the two-car garage and turned off the car. *It was carpeted. The damn garage was carpeted.* Rosie straightened. It could only get worse from here on.

He was putting his key in the lock when she remembered. She slapped her forehead, and the clip holding her hair up on one side fell out.

'Kent, I forgot to tell you! I found Gardenia. And I was right. She was in my dream. Not exactly the same, of course, but near enough.'

Kent bent to pick up the fallen clip and handed it to her. She stuffed it back in her hair.

'Does that mean what I think it means?' he asked, turning the key and opening the door for her. She stepped in and he took her elbow, leading her the few steps to the kitchen, then flicked on some soft, indirect lighting.

'I don't know. What do you think it means?'

'That she works for Beachline.'

Rosie smiled. 'She does.'

'And?'

'And what?'

'And, as in who *is* it?' he asked.

Rosie pursed her lips. She'd known he was going to ask, and she'd already decided not to tell him. The matter was resolved. She reached into her tote bag and pulled out the remaining letters. They were wrapped in green silk with a darker green ribbon. The color of Kent's eyes, Gardenia had said. She was right.

'Here.' She handed him the letters.

'What's this?' He turned the silk-wrapped package over in his hand.

'The rest of the letters. Gardenia and I had a long talk. She was pretty scared at being found out and promised you won't be hearing from her again. And just to put your mind at rest, she's no threat. Kind of nice, really. She just let her, uh, admiration for you get a bit out of hand, is all.' Rosie looked into his intense eyes and empathized completely.

He eyed her with male wariness. 'You're not going to tell me, are you?'

'Nope.' She crossed her arms and leaned against a counter clad in a coat of shining stainless steel. 'I'm going to leave you with the mystery, the possibility that every woman currently working at Beachline is in love with you. It'll do wonders for that malnourished ego of yours,' she quipped. *And I'll be keeping my word to Gardenia*, she added mentally.

He seemed to consider this, then tossed the letters casually onto the smooth laminated table occupying the middle of the room. Briefly, he rubbed at his chin, but he didn't smile.

Finally, he gazed down at her. 'I don't want every woman at Beachline to be in love with me. I only want you.' He cradled her neck in his strong hand and pulled her to his chest. 'I want *you* to love me, Rosie.'

She gaped at him, wondering what had

160

happened to all the air in the room. There'd been plenty moments ago. 'Don't say that,' she instructed him lamely.

He wanted her to love him, the foolish man. Didn't he know she already did? Okay, maybe she hadn't admitted it, even to herself, but after last night—and today—what else could it be except love? She was flaming nuts about him. But she needed to understand why he'd gone to so much trouble to get her to the barbecue and meet his family. She'd wanted to believe it was a change of heart, a softening to the idea of a big family. But she couldn't be sure. And until she was, love was out of the question.

His hand heated her neck. His face was far too close to hers. Kissing distance. His lips seemed to soften as she looked at them, subtly prepared to meet hers.

No.

If she kissed him she was roadkill! She jerked back and the comb fell out of her hair again. This time they both bent to pick it up and they bumped heads.

Kent let out a breath, massaged the crash site, then shook his head. 'Okay, Rosie. How about that coffee? We'll save the hard stuff for later.'

'I don't drink liquor.'

'I meant conversation. After what happened last night, you and I need to talk.'

She amazed herself. Her face didn't heat.

Finally, the pilot light on her blush furnace had burned itself out.

About time. She'd been hot faced since this man had walked into her messy life.

'Okay,' she said. 'I'm up for some coffee—and talk.' She searched out the coffeepot, wanting to make herself useful and to get out from under Kent's speculative gaze. No use pushing her luck on the blush business.

She glanced around his spotless kitchen, its steel, laminate, and chrome surfaces all gleaming coolly under the indirect lighting. Not a basket, a spice, or a mismatched mug in the place. Or a dog hair. 'Where's Lacy? she asked. 'I thought you had an Irish wolfhound.' She spotted a black coffeepot tucked away in a corner and headed for it.

Kent took the coffeepot from her hands. 'I'll do that,' he said. 'And Lacy's at kennel care.'

'Kennel care? Is that like daycare for dogs?'

'Uh-huh.' He filled the coffeepot's well with water and measured coffee into the filter. 'I drop her off every morning before I go to work and pick her up on my way home. She needs the exercise. I never leave her cooped up here all day. I made special arrangements for them to keep her tonight, because of the barbecue.'

'Why do you have her if she can't be with you?'

He stroked his cheek with an index finger, then shrugged. 'She's good company.'

And you can't face this ice palace without her,

162

Rosie finished for him. Her heart smiled. Anyone who *needed* a dog wasn't completely irredeemable.

Kent finished with the coffee-making and reached for her hand. 'Let's go into the living room.'

Leather, of course, the color of wet sand. She didn't like leather much; it always made her bottom cold. She sat down and wriggled deep into the sofa to get some warmth. 'Nice,' she fibbed, running her hand over the smooth, luxurious leather. It felt surprisingly sensuous, like healthy skin over relaxed muscle. Kent after lovemaking. Sex. All she could think about was sex. Maybe she should enter a treatment program.

'Glad you like it. Jayne took care of the decorating for me.' He looked around, then looked puzzled. 'She said this room captured me perfectly.'

Rosie caressed the edge of her cushion again. 'She was right.'

Kent sat beside her and put his feet up on the oak and iron coffee table. He draped an arm around the back of the sofa, which placed his hand perilously close to her ear, but he didn't touch her.

'Rosie, I know you're tired, but about today—' He stopped as though he were looking for a sign, telling him which way to go. 'I know I wasn't exactly honest in the way I got you there, but I wanted you to meet my

163

family.'

'Why?'

'Good question.' He stopped as if to sort through his thoughts. 'I thought it was all about making you change your mind.'

'Run that by me again.'

'I figured if you saw what living, breathing chaos, looked like, you'd reconsider the size of your proposed contribution to the nation's birthrate. Then . . .'

The thin flame of hope in Rosie's heart sputtered but held. 'Then?'

He shifted closer, lifted the hair from her nape, and let it sift through his fingers until it settled back against her shoulders. She tingled like crystal tapped by a silver spoon.

'Then,' he whispered against her throat. 'It got complicated.' His breath against her skin came in small, hot gusts and his voice was husky. Come to think of it, her own breathing was a bit on the restless side.

He kissed her cheek, just under her jaw, then her throat. 'No sex, remember?' she said, arching her neck so he had more room. *So, what's this, O'Hanlon, a cooking lesson?* Lady Brain intoned.

'I remember,' he murmured, pushing her top aside and kissing that delightfully tender spot between shoulder and neck. 'You have the most incredible skin. Have I told you that?' He drew one finger along the front edge of her scooped-necked tee, then bent to kiss her just above the cleft between her breasts. 'Incredible.'

His lips skimmed the top of her breasts, kissing here softly, there more firmly. His hand clasped her waist, pulled her closer. Damned if her body wasn't going on auto pilot. Damned if her breasts weren't heaving with enough thrust to power an outboard. Damned if she wasn't the craziest woman on five continents. 'No sex.' She croaked with conviction forged from spider webs and cotton candy.

Kent went still. 'Do you want me to stop?' he asked, his lips a hair's-breadth from her nipple.

Her body thrumming with need, Rosie lifted his head, and looked into his silky green eyes. He meant it, she could see that. He'd stop if she wanted him to, and, of course, it made her love him even more, want him even more. She grinned. 'If you do, Summerton, I won't be held responsible for the consequences.'

His eyes gleamed. He stood and pulled her to her feet. 'Come on, Red. Tonight we'll test-drive my bed.' He looked at the couch. 'I'm not a big fan of leather.'

CHAPTER ELEVEN

Kent woke up guilty.

He looked at his bedside clock. Already after seven. He'd meant to talk to Rosie last night, get some kind of consensus, or, better yet, a compromise on this big family thing. Instead, they'd made love until they were both exhausted.

The only serious discussion had been some inconclusive pillow talk about whether to spay Lacy or pair her up with Font. What the hell they'd do with a litter of Irish wolfhounds, Kent had no idea, but the idea seemed to set Rosie on fire. Looked like the woman wanted as many dogs as she did kids. Things were going from bad to worse, and he hadn't even broached the subject of the two of them becoming a serious *us*.

He looked at the woman snuggled into the pillow next to him, and his chest constricted. And it was more than lust, it was love. Suddenly, he couldn't imagine his life without her. Trouble was he didn't know where to go from here, or even if there was a place to go. But somehow he had to keep Rosie O'Hanlon in his life.

He got up and padded toward the bathroom. He'd shower and think about it. There had to be a way. The differences between him and Rosie had to be sorted out—and soon. And, much as he'd like to ignore it and pretend it didn't matter, the issue of how many kids a couple wanted was incredibly important—and thorny as hell. Not only did he not want a zillion kids, he didn't have time for them. For the next few years, running Beachline was going to take all the energy he had.

He turned on the shower. He was fortunate that Rosie occasionally changed her mind. His lips twitched to a smile. Like last night.

By the time the water was streaming down his back, he was optimistic. By the time he'd shaved and dressed, he was enthusiastic. They'd talk it through, he'd take her to the family brunch, and they'd work it out. No problem. All it took was compromise. Rosie would just have to understand his work schedule.

* * *

Rosie was in the kitchen ferreting through his cupboards when he got there. She was wearing his terry bathrobe, which unfortunately shrouded every feminine curve on her body, and her brilliant hair was wet and slicked to her head.

When she saw him, she looked up, pulled at the collar of the robe, and smiled. 'Hope you don't mind. I used the other bathroom.'

He walked up and pulled her loosely into his arms. 'Use anything you like,' he said, kissing her wet head. 'What's mine is yours.'

She tilted her head, gave him a sassy look, and stroked him boldly. 'What a nice thought.'

Kent gasped for air. He took her hands and lifted them to his chest. 'You could be addictive, you know that?'

She locked her arms around his neck. 'I wish,' she murmured, then pulled his face to hers and kissed him fiercely. There was an unsettling desperation in the kiss which Kent didn't understand. Puzzled, he pulled back and looked down at her.

She dropped her gaze and stepped out of his arms. 'I'm going to get dressed.' She gestured toward the gurgling coffeepot. 'Coffee's almost ready.' At the door she turned back. 'Oh, and Con called when you were in the shower. He's your business partner, right?'

'Uh huh.'

'Said he was on his way.' With that she left the room.

Con was coming. Here. Now. He'd have been less surprised if she'd announced the imminent arrival of the King of Borneo, her adopted country.

'Con . . .' Kent muttered, pouring himself a cup of coffee. Wouldn't you know it? The man Kent most wanted to see was about to arrive at a singularly inopportune moment—unless he could head him off. He quickly set his coffee

168

on the counter, picked up the phone, and dialed Con's cell number. He'd barely keyed the last digit before the door chimed. Too late.

Kent opened the door and Con stepped in with purpose, his stride long, and his face grim. 'We need to talk,' he said tersely.

'After you,' Kent said, closing the door and waving an arm in the direction of the kitchen. 'But you should know your timing's lousy.'

'As far as you're concerned everything I do is lousy, so what's new?'

Kent had no idea what he was talking about and didn't bother to ask. Con was a master of the cryptic comment, as good at them as he was at pulling his disappearing act.

'I've been trying to get hold of you for weeks,' he said. 'Hawaii was one thing, but, damn it, Con, we have a business to run. Where in hell have you been?'

'Trying to find a buyer for my Beachline shares.'

Kent's head shot up. 'What are you talking about?'

Con ignored him. 'And I've got one. Here's the deal. Either you buy me out, according to our partnership agreement, or I sell to the Turfside group.'

'Turfside?' Shocked to his bones, Kent stared at his partner and tried to put his thoughts into some kind of order. He hadn't known what to expect from Con's sudden visit, but it sure as hell wasn't this. Turfside was a conglomerate, a big player in the golf course management business, and the last partner in the world either he or Beachline needed. Beachline Resort was a hell of a lot more than a mere golf course. And Con knew that. What was going on here? He stared at his partner, a partner he thought was his friend. None of this computed.

*   *   *

Rosie heard voices in the kitchen, hesitated about going in, but plunged ahead anyway. She needed a caffeine jolt.

'Hi.' Rosie said, dropping her tote on the table and heading for the coffee. She glanced at the two grim-faced men and noticed the room temperature. Cold. Very cold. Her smile slipped. 'Oh-oh, I think an "oops" is in order here. Why don't I make myself scarce?' She edged toward the door.

'Rosie, this is Conrad York,' Kent said.

She smiled at the man. Good looking, but in a miserable mood, judging from the tic in his jaw. He nodded at her distractedly but didn't return her smile.

'Rosie,' Kent said. 'Why don't you wait in the—'

Con interrupted. 'No need for that. I'm leaving.' He gave Kent a hard look. 'I've said what I came to say. No use prolonging it.' He smiled wryly. 'My lawyer will be in touch with yours, Kent. The way I see it, the sooner we end this charade of a partnership, the better.'

Rosie was fascinated. She wouldn't leave now, no matter what. Nosiness was another of her many virtues.

Con was nearly out of the kitchen when Kent spoke, his voice hard, his expression unreadable. 'Hold it right there, Con. Not one more damn step until you give me an explanation. You owe me that.'

Con swiveled, as if he were wired to blow. Then he took a deep breath. 'Okay. How about this? When we bought Beachline, it was a partnership. I was perfectly willing to do my share and more. Back then we worked together.' He shot Kent a cold look. 'But now? You're a one-man band, Summerton, and you like it that way. If you don't trust me enough to do my job, I'm outta there. Plain and simple. I don't need you, or anyone else, second-guessing every damn decision I make.'

'Second-guessing . . . ?' Kent looked puzzled, but his eyes blazed. 'You've barely showed up for work in the past three months. What the hell was I supposed to do?'

'You don't get it, do you?' Con said, glaring at Kent. 'There wasn't anything for me to show up for.'

Rosie put down her coffee. She was beginning to get the drift of what was going on here, and it didn't look good for Kent. For the briefest moment, Con's anger dissipated, and

Rosie saw regret in his eyes.

'But you were there every day, right? And every night? And probably most weekends.'

Kent nodded crisply. 'Damn straight. Someone had to be.'

'Did it ever occur to you that on occasion I would have liked that someone to be me—without you looking over my shoulder? If you'd trusted my judgment occasionally, relied on me—' He swore, dropped his head briefly, then lifted it again. 'Forget it. The truth is you're a control freak, Summerton. Beachline and you will make the perfect couple.' He headed for the door in long, purposeful strides. In seconds the door slammed, and he was gone.

Silence.

'Ouch,' Rosie said.

Kent didn't answer her, just stood there staring at the door his partner had gone through as if in shock. Then he slammed the mug he'd been holding down on the counter. Coffee slopped over the stainless steel top.

He looked at her, but his gaze was frigid. 'Do you want something to eat? I don't have much, but I can rustle something up.'

'Excuse me? Didn't your business partner just walk out of here? And didn't he just dump all over you because you wouldn't let him do his job? And isn't your life more or less in danger of falling apart?'

He straightened and headed for the

refrigerator. 'I'll deal with it. How about some eggs?'

'Forget the damned eggs!' Rosie narrowed her gaze. 'How are you going to deal with it?'

'It's not your concern, Rosie.'

'Is that the same as "mind your own business"?'

'Yes. Look, I've been managing Beachline for months with no help from Con York. His leaving just simplifies things.'

Rosie ignored the fact he'd told her to mind her own business. She generally ignored stupidity. 'You're exhausted. You sleep like a sentry on the front line. You have no life. You're in danger of going up in flames from executive burnout—' she glared at him '—and you think your partner's leaving simplifies things? Your neurons aren't firing, Summerton.' She put her hands on her hips and tried to look threatening. 'Go after him.'

'*Go after*—are you nuts?' The look he gave her—half anger, half incredulity—said he thought she was.

'Okay, ready up then. I've got something to say, and I want you to listen carefully. You and I have got something happening here—'

She took a deep breath. What she needed now was attitude, and plenty of it, because Rosie O'Hanlon was about to put her heart on the line. She marched out on her wobbly limb.

'Like I said, we've got something happening here, and it's all your doing. I told you in the

173

beginning I wasn't interested in a hyperactive workaholic as the father of my children—and I told you I want a lot of children.' She thinned her lips a moment. 'And I do. Nothing's changed. But would you let it go? Let me go? No. You ate, slept, smiled, and seduced your way into my heart. You even took me to meet your mother.'

And that really made her mad. When she began pacing, Kent followed her moves in open fascination.

'Then you brought me here last night so we could talk.' She snorted. 'Some talk!'

'We were busy,' he said calmly, lifting a dark brow. 'And as I recall, you weren't complaining,'

'Neither were you,' she shot back.

'No, I wasn't.' He almost smiled. 'I could make love to you forever, Rosie.'

She blinked, then decided to ignore the sparkle in her heart, the swoosh in her tummy—and his last remark. He had a way of getting her off course. Not this time.

'Where was I?' she asked.

'I can't be sure, but I think you were telling me I had to chase my partner down and beg him to come back because I had you meet my mother.' He leaned against the counter and crossed his arms. 'I know there's logic in there somewhere. I just haven't been able to follow it.'

Rosie hesitated, but only for a nanosecond.

'Okay, let's start over again—'

'Good idea.'

She frowned so deeply she felt the lines interlace on her forehead. Was she actually in love with this irritating man? It didn't bear thinking about. 'Like I said, we have something happening between us—and the way I see it, you were the main instigator of it. Before you stomped up onto my front porch, huffing and puffing about some poor woman writing you naughty letters, I had an orderly life.'

Kent looked puzzled, as if the assimilation of Rosie and an orderly life was too taxing to contemplate.

She went on. 'I was happy. I had a dog, a house, a computer with which to eke out my meager living, and a plan. Then you came along and ruined everything.'

'Something happened to Font?' he asked dryly.

'Don't be smart, you know what I mean. You ruined my plan, treated it as if it were so much cow dung.'

'Cow dung.'

'I was going to be smart for a change, quit wasting my time on ambitious suits, find a man who had some . . . perspective enough to put home and kids before profit and loss.'

Tears massed behind her eyelids, and she forced them back. 'But would you leave me alone? No. You had to go and make me fall in love with you.'

'Rosie.' Kent moved away from the counter and toward her. She stepped back.

The tears seeped through, and she smeared them away with the back of her hand.

'No. Don't even think about holding me. Don't you get it, Summerton? I don't want to love a man who wants to work a hundred hours a week. My dad did that, and he had the heart attack to prove it.'

'I'm sorry,' Kent said quietly.

'Ancient history now. I was four.' She sniffed, not wanting sympathy. 'I scarcely remember him. What I do remember is that after he died, Mom had to take over as breadwinner. She worked as hard as he did.' She looked up at Kent and for a moment was lost in the intensity of his gaze. Then she straightened. She wasn't one for spending too much time in the past, but she sure intended to learn from it and stack life's chaotic deck in favor of the family she planned in whatever way she could.

'I'm not your dad, Rosie,' Kent said. 'And there's nothing wrong with enjoying your work.'

She stared at him, studied him, tried to change her mind and tell herself she was wrong about him. 'No, there's nothing wrong with enjoying your work, but there's a lot wrong with being addicted to it. When it makes you exclude others, when you can't let it

176

go—even enough to share the load with your partner, I think that makes you ambitious . . . to a fault.'

She picked up her wrecked tote bag and headed for the door.

'You can't be leaving.' He looked stunned.

She turned back and smiled through her tears. 'I'm going back to Borneo, hotshot. And this time I'll be staying.' She saw his mouth tighten, his chin set to a stubborn line, and she saw the hurt in his eyes.

'You're serious.'

'Never more so.'

'Fine. I'll get my keys and drive you.' His words came hard and fast. He pushed away from the counter he was leaning against.

Rosie quickly shook her head. 'No, thanks. I'll take a cab to Beachline and pick up my car.'

'I said I'll drive you.'

'And I said, you won't.'

He glared at her. She glared back. No way was Rosaleen Fiona O'Hanlon going to get within whiff distance of this man's aftershave ever again. The fat lady had definitely sung.

It was over.

CHAPTER TWELVE

Kent stood stone-stiff for a long time. He felt as if he'd been through a flak attack. First Con, then Rosie.

Rosie was gone.

He closed his eyes, and cursed. Damned if his eyes weren't watering. For want of anything better to do, but finally having to do something, he walked to the sink and ran a cold glass of water. He tried to piece events together, make sense of her leaving. One minute she was in his arms—then Con had come and gone—and the next minute she was out the door. He drained the water glass.

Maybe she was right. Maybe it was for the best. Sometimes two people were just wrong for each other, and there was no fixing it or forcing it. She was definitely right when she accused him of not letting her go. But she'd been straight with him from the beginning, made it absolutely clear that she didn't want to mess around in a go-nowhere relationship—which he had to admit was his starting point. Even when she'd told him she wanted to settle down and have a family—a very large family— he hadn't stopped. Any sane man would have hit the ground running.

His stomach knotted and he rubbed it, but truth was a tightrope. And the truth was, he hadn't been in his right mind since she'd opened her front door that first day, wearing broken glasses and those crazy checkered socks. And after that first bowl of soup, when she'd tried to fix him up with her accountant, he'd been had.

Abruptly he shoved away from the counter.

What the hell did she want, anyway? Some male version of Martha Stewart, who'd muck out the storm drains in the morning and make cobble shoes for the kids at night? Where in hell did that leave Beachline? He had a big commitment there. And with Con leaving—

He stood there, holding the water glass loosely in one hand, rubbing the back of his neck with the other. It was as if he didn't know which move to make next.

With Con leaving for good, there was no hope for a letup in his workload. His lips curved to a pained smile at the irony of it. Rosie had walked out because he wouldn't give more of himself, and Con walked out because he wouldn't give less.

Well, tough! He slammed the water glass into the sink. It cracked, and a sharp wedge of glass leapt from the sink to the counter top. He left it there. Who the hell cared, anyway? Just who the hell cared?

I like my work, and damn it, I don't have time for a houseful of kids. He and Rosie were both better off with other partners. And he sure as hell was better off without making commitments he couldn't keep.

He glanced at his watch. Nine-thirty. There was one place he was still welcome. At his desk. He slapped his head.

The damn brunch.

He couldn't not show, but if he were lucky, he'd get in an hour's work before his family arrived. Hell, maybe he'd do exactly what Rosie would expect him to do—work right through it. As it stood now, there wasn't a damn soul who'd care anyway. On that fine, uplifting note of blatant self-pity, he grabbed a jacket, his keys, and headed for his Saab.

*   *   *

Rosie turned into her driveway, glad to be home. She needed to be alone, lick her emotional wounds, but it wasn't to be. That was definitely Jonesy's Sundancer cozied up to her front step. She sighed, pulled her Geo to a stop behind Jonesy's car, and sat there like the dummy she was.

She wanted to cry, a full-out caterwaul that would carry into the next county. And she wanted Kent Summerton with an ache that made open heart surgery seem restful.

She forced herself out of the car and made it to the first step. But instead of stepping on it, she sat down, deciding to pull herself together before she faced Jonesy. She picked up a rock, turned it over in her hand, and tossed it—hard. It didn't bounce, but settled willingly into a new patch of dirt. Stupid rock.

Stupid Rosie!

She'd done exactly what she said she wouldn't do. Fallen in love with the wrong man. And she'd even thought it through this time, developed a plan of sorts. And where did it get her? Sitting here throwing rocks. Too bad she couldn't drop a few down the hole in her brain. Fill up the blank space.

There was no hope for her. She was a muddled, redheaded fool of a woman, and she couldn't help it. Didn't bode well for her future kids. She probably had terrible genes, some inborn neediness that would make all her daughters-to-be pushovers for politicians and criminals.

Font barked from inside the house. She'd been spotted.

She stood, took a step up, surveyed her pastoral domain, and swiped at the bit of moisture tickling her cheeks. Maybe she did get off track occasionally, jump too fast at too little. For instance, writing those dumb love letters. Why had that even seemed like a good idea? But she knew one thing—how you made your living in life was a distant second to how you chose to live it. She had a hard time seeing anyone standing at the Pearly Gates begging for just one more staff meeting. Couldn't Kent see that? Damn his workaholic hide. Why couldn't he get his priorities straight?

Rosie didn't move for a moment, then tugged at her hair. Was that really her railing about priorities again?

No. That was a desperate woman looking for words to mend a heartache. She turned and headed up the stairs to the house.

After a rousing reunion with Font, during which he managed to lick her forehead, and she hugged him so tight that he yelped, she strolled into the kitchen, determined to be cool and nonchalant. She would not bleed, figuratively speaking, all over her clean kitchen floor.

Jonesy, wearing Rosie's favorite scarlet bathrobe, was at the sink filling a kettle with water.

'What are you doing?' Rosie asked. She dropped her tote on the wing chair near the fireplace and tried to sidestep Font's tail, still whipping about with enough force to bruise.

'Making tea. Where are your bags?' Jonesy said, then looked at her. 'Other than the ones under your bloodshot eyes, I mean.'

'Very funny.' Rosie took the kettle out of Jonesy's hand. 'Sit down. I'll make you some tea. *You* tell me what you're doing here.'

Jonesy yawned. 'I came to walk Font last night because you called and asked me to— remember? Then I just kind of fell asleep on your sofa.'

'In my best robe?'

Jonesy smiled. 'What are friends for?

182

Besides, it's a terrible color for you. The fashion police said so.'

'Hm-m.' Rosie said absently. She didn't really care about her robe. Her carping was only a momentary diversion to distract her from the pain in her heart.

'Now for the real question,' Jonesy said. 'What are you doing here? I figured you were locked in the arms of love.'

'I live here, dontcha know?' Rosie quipped. Then with the kettle set to boil, she leaned against the counter, stroked Font's bristly gray head, and tried to grin. Damn, but this smiling-through-your-tears bit was tough.

Jonesy tilted her head, narrowed her gaze, and made a sound that was a curious cross between Harrumph and Ha. 'Judging from that non-answer, my guess is you blew it,' she accused, with what Rosie read as an evil grin. At the very least, it was a know-it-all grin. Same thing.

'I did not blow it. Kent Summerton did—'

'I'll bet he was good at it, too.'

'Jonesy!' Rosie tried to be stern, but she couldn't quite squash a fleeting grin. Then she sobered. 'He took me to meet his family,' she complained.

'The bastard.'

'He said he wanted to talk about us. But his partner arrived and then walked out on him because he's fed up with Kent not letting him do his job, and Kent wouldn't give him another

183

chance, which means Kent will have to work even harder than he does now, which means he won't have time for . . . anything. Let alone me and the kids.'

'Rosie, I hate to tell you this, but you don't have any kids.'

'He's a work addict, Jonesy. I don't want that. I want a husband, a blue-ribbon dad, and a family—a big family—that comes before anything. *Anything!*' She was going to cry. She sniffed hard and held her nose as though she were going to sneeze. Font nuzzled her other hand with his cold nose and leaned against her leg. She was *not* going to cry.

'Sure you do.' Jonesy came up beside her and put an arm around her shoulders. 'And you're going to have it. You've still got your plan, haven't you?' Jonesy patted her shoulder kindly.

Jonesy's voice was too soft, too soothing. 'You know, the one about dating every man on the North American continent until you find one who'll put his hand up, certify he has the appropriate sperm count, then guarantee you exactly the life you want.'

Rosie's hackles rose. 'So what's wrong with that?'

'I'd say your crazy plan has as much chance of finding you a man as *Cyrano Inc.* has of paying for a month's supply of toothpicks.' Jonesy dropped her hand from Rosie's shoulder. 'Ever consider that maybe you can't

184

think straight when it comes to Kent Summerton, Rosie?'

Rosie glared at her.

'Don't glower at me. I'm right and you know it. You just listen up, Rosaleen Fiona O'Hanlon.'

When Jonesy started tapping her thumb against the index finger of her opposite hand, Rosaleen knew she was in for a lecture. 'He's a hardworking man, and you hold it against him. He doesn't want a dozen kids—' Jonesy gave her a slanted look '—but then, who in this day and age does? You hold that against him. He takes you to meet his family, and you give him another bad mark.' Jonesy tapped the final finger. 'The man has knocked himself out trying to get your attention, and you're mad about that. God help him if he ever brings you flowers.'

Rosie puckered her mouth and bit on her lower lip. Jonesy's finger-counted list did make her slightly uncomfortable. Her best friend seemed to think that she was unreasonable. No. Not Rosie O'Hanlon. She was the most reasonable of beings. Wasn't she?

She felt Jonesy's hand grip her shoulder, squeeze. 'He loves you, Rosaleen. And you love him. Make it work.'

Rosie looked at her friend. 'Are you suggesting what I think you're suggesting?'

'Yes. Compromise.'

'Yuck. I hate that word.' She brushed a

damp spot on her cheek and dropped her hand. Font licked it and gave her a pleading look. She could swear he knew about her and Kent's plans for him and Lacy. Was he mourning the loss of a litter he'd dreamed about?

'I said compromise, Rosie, not cave in. There's a big difference.'

Rosie wasn't so sure, but she didn't want to talk about it any more. 'I'll think about it.'

'Good, now let's eat. I'm starved.'

*　　　*　　　*

'You look good,' Mike said, stepping up to Kent at the buffet table. His tone as dry as the toast he plucked from the long, food-laden table. 'Kind of like the last artifact up from the Titanic.'

'Thanks.' Kent said. He picked up a plate and stared at the food. He didn't want any of it, but if he didn't eat, he'd never hear the end of it. He dug in.

He still couldn't figure out why he was even here. He should be at his desk. That's what he'd planned. But when he'd stepped into his office this morning, the silence, the neat desk, the brooding computer, and all those sparkling windows overlooking his precious investment property had felt as welcoming as a prisoner's holding cell.

Then he'd heard a faint rustling sound. Con

was in the next office, clearing out his desk. That did it.

Kent had walked out then and there. And he must have looked damn strange, striding down the hall. Mae Smythe had gaped at him, and so had Susan Lyle. Too bad, he'd needed some air. He'd needed to *not* think about Rosie. By the time he got back from his not-thinking trek, his family was spread out along the east patio. And somehow, he hadn't been able to get away—make that tear himself away—since.

'Where's Rosie?' Mike asked, eyeing Kent's full-to-capacity plate. 'I figured she'd be here today.'

'Home, I guess.' Kent piled some kind of egg soufflé thing on top of roast beef, pickles, and baked beans.

Mike grimaced. 'You blew it, didn't you?'

'Blew what?' Kent stalked the table, added a bun before picking four strips of crisp bacon to add to his plate. And Rosie said he didn't eat right. If only she could see him now. *If only he could see her.*

'Rosie. The romance thing.'

Kent glared at his brother. 'Give it up, Mike. I don't want to talk about it.'

After a brief silence, Mike said, 'Okay,' and took his place beside Kent.

Kent stared at his plate as if seeing it for the first time; his stomach rolled. He shoved the plate aside and downed some orange juice.

'She thinks I work too much.'

'You do,' Mike said, before forking in some hash browns.

'She wants a zillion kids.'

'So?' Mike waved his empty fork around the patio, encompassing Mom, Dad, their eight other siblings, their wives and husbands and all their kids. 'She'll fit right in.'

Kent followed Mike's gesture and let out a breath. 'You don't get it. None of you get it. I don't want that kind of confusion. I want—'

'Your own room, your own toys, and a brand new shirt with store creases in it. Something. Anything that hasn't passed through nine sets of hands before it lands in yours.'

What the hell was Mike trying to say? Kent wasn't talking about his childhood, damn it. He opened his mouth to argue, then shut it again, strangely disturbed. Then again, maybe he was.

'I know the feeling.' Mike went on. 'Only in my case, being close to the top of the pecking order, most of the stuff passed through only a quarter of the hands yours did. It was hell, though.' He smiled. 'I used to dream about my own place, neat bookshelves, my own football—' He stopped. 'And I got it, too. Then I met Leona, and she ruined everything.'

'I don't get it. I thought everything was going great between you two.' Kent felt a keen disappointment. He'd always thought his brother and Leona were happily married. Just

188

proved his case. The strain of too many offspring was taking its inevitable toll.

Mike rolled his eyes. 'I never thought of you as the slow one, Kent. I was joking. But let me put it in terms you'll understand. I'd rather have Leona, my boys, and those twin girls over there—' he gestured to the long table, where Leona was helping Emma and Jane with their plates '—than any moldy old football. You got it, bro?'

Kent rotated his chair so he faced the buffet table. His attention fixed on the girls, captured by the intense effort they were making to balance their plates and navigate between the adult giants to where he and Mike sat. Both of them had their tongues tucked firmly into the edge of their lips. Their concentration was total. Taking one careful step at a time, they were almost there.

'Zach, don't!' Jayne yelled.

Kent turned in time to see Zach hurtling toward them with a balloon flying above his head. His eyes fixed on it, he sideswiped both girls from the rear within inches of Kent's knees. They didn't stand a chance. Neither did their plates. Kent lifted his hands to provide a break, but he was too late.

They hit him in two waves; eggs, ketchup, and jam first, followed immediately by two shocked little girls, driven with enough force to embed the brunch food into his white shirt and slacks. He caught both of them in his arms, then toppled backward in an ungainly heap of egg stains, flailing arms, broken glass, flying legs, and screeches that sounded as if they came from monkeys being boiled in oil.

As he and the crying girls scrambled to their feet, the family gathered around—all of them talking at once.

Emma pointed at him and shrieked, 'Unken Ken's blooding.'

He touched his forehead. He was 'blooding.'

'Let me see that,' Jayne said, pushing through the cast of thousands that was his family. She mopped at it with a clean linen napkin, held it to the cut, then announced, 'Somebody get a bandage. It's only a scratch. He'll live.' She replaced her hand on the napkin with Kent's and turned to her son Zach. 'As for you, kiddo . . .'

While Zach received lecture one thousand and one about looking where he was going, Kent pressed the napkin to his head and pulled his sticky shirt away from his chest. Jane and Emma, having wailed themselves out, only to discover they were unhurt, now eyed him with awe and speculation. His mother drummed up ointment and a bandage from the magic sack she called her handbag, and cleaned up his head. The girls watched avidly.

When his mother was done fussing over him, he smiled at the girls and held out his arms. They clambered onto his knees. The three of them looked as if they'd been rolled in finger paints.

Emma touched his bandage. 'Bad ouchie,' she said solemnly. When she drew her finger away, Jane copied her action. The touch of their small fingers was like the kiss of a butterfly. They were obviously enthralled by bandages.

'It's okay,' he said. 'How about you? You okay?'

'Uh-huh.' They nodded in unison. 'Mommy says you a hairo.'

'She does, does she?' He kissed each of them on their silky blond heads. 'Well, that's good, because I've always wanted to be a "hairo."'

'Mine kiss it better?' Jane asked soberly, pointing to his battle wound.

'Definitely. It's exactly what it needs.' He leaned his head forward, and both girls planted soft kisses on his bandage. Even with their nursing duties done, they stuck by him, giving him hugs and patting his hand, until they were carted off by their mom for face washing and general cleanup.

He watched them go, his fingers tracing the line of his bandage. The line of their curative smooch. Some 'hairo' he was. He was as mushy inside as a week-old plum.

'There's not a balance sheet in this world that can give you that.' Mike said from somewhere behind him. 'Even if they do lose your football and mess up your bookshelves.'

He looked at his brother. The man was a sage. Because he was right. Absolutely right.

He stood so quickly his head spun, not quite sure of his next move. Rosie. He had to speak to Rosie. He cursed. The woman never wanted to see him again. Well, too bad, because he'd decided to see her. And he had some bigtime convincing to do. It was show-and-tell time.

First he had to talk to Con.

'Mike, I'm going to talk to my business partner for a while, but I want you to do something for me . . .'

*   *   *

Rosie sat on the top porch step, rubbing Font's ear and watching the dust storm made by Jonesy's black Sundancer as it disappeared down the road. Finally, she had what she wanted. She was alone.

She hated it. Sometimes it felt as though she'd always been alone.

She brushed angrily at a threatening tear. Oh, great, just because she'd spent a few hours with Kent's wonderful family, she was going to start feeling sorry for herself? No way. She had a pretty good life. No. Make that a great life. Her mom was the best. She had the farmhouse. Font. A good job. Everything was just fine, thank you very much. So she was underinventoried in the family department. So be it. She'd have her own family. Her own kids.

Someday.

Trouble was, now she wanted those kids to look like their dad, and she wanted that dad to be Kent Summerton. She took a tissue from her jeans pocket and blew her nose. What she *did not* want was a man who worked as though the financial health of corporate America relied on an injection of his blood on an hourly basis. She blew her nose again. Damn hay fever. Yeah, sure.

She stood, leaned against the porch rail, and looked across her sunlit pasture. Everything about Kent was so confusing, it made her head hurt. On one hand, she respected his ambition, his drive. She'd want her kids to have those traits, too. But on the other, knowing when to ease up, when to come home, and *be home* in body and soul was lots more important. And then there was the baby count. They couldn't even agree on that.

Maybe she could compromise . . .

She shuddered. Lord, if prioritizing was rubber gloves and suction, compromise was scalpels and clamps. But was she so selfish, so stubborn she couldn't even think about it? Could she sit back and lose Kent because her obstinacy button was stuck on max?

She held the tissue to her nose and shut her eyes. She'd already lost him, walked out in fine fettle. And he'd let her go. Fettles and all.

She'd have to learn to live with it. But oh, how her heart ached, cried in her chest like a cold, starving orphan.

Font butted her thigh with his big head and whimpered. She scratched his head. 'You wouldn't be sticking by me, friend, if you knew that in the process of screwing up my love life, I also screwed up yours.'

Font wagged his tail, proving that ignorance was indeed bliss.

She smiled, but her lips had trouble holding the curve. 'Come on, big guy, let's go in. I've got a new cookbook called *Dinners For One.* I can't wait to try it.'

She heard the first horn blast when her hand was on the door knob. Then a second, more insistent. But it was the cacophony of a dozen or more that finally got her attention. She turned to see a cavalcade of cars kicking up dust on the road beyond her fence. Horns continued to blare as the noisy parade roared down her driveway. A dozen cars. More.

A black Saab was in the lead.

The cars' horns sounded until Kent pulled up to her porch and jumped out of his car, followed immediately by an Irish wolfhound the size of a pony. Font bolted down the stairs to sniff out the situation. This left Rosie alone on the porch, first gaping at the crowd, then staring at Kent, hope growing in her chest like a weed on steroids.

Kent cleared the steps two at time, took her in his arms, and kissed her until her vision clouded. She still couldn't find her voice, which was just as well because she'd probably say something of monumental idiocy and spoil the whole dream. And this had to be a dream.

Car doors opened, and Kent's entire family spilled into her yard, most of them wearing smiles a mile wide. Kent's mother waved. So did Jayne, Zach, and the twins.

She waved back weakly and tried to make sense of things. Not easy after she'd just been kissed by the world's leading osculation expert.

'Everybody's here,' she mumbled, clutching Kent's shoulders.

'I invited them.'

'Why?'

'Because they're family and because family is what this is all about.' He touched her face, smiled. 'Besides, I figure you'll think twice about throwing me off the porch with a cast of thousands to watch.'

Rosie didn't get it, but one thing was certain. She wasn't the least inclined to throw him off the porch. Although she'd super-glue her teeth shut before she let him know that. At least until she heard what he had to say.

When she smiled into the crowd and waved again, they moved en masse toward the porch steps, like a throng of movie extras called to the staging area.

'Rosie,' Kent said, 'Look at me.'

Still dazed, she looked into a pair of sexy green eyes now hot with intensity.

'I can't let you go. I won't let you go.'

'But—' she started, feeling she should protest, but unclear as to why.

'No buts.' Kent said firmly. 'We're two intelligent people, and we can work this thing out, given time and a compromise or two.'

Compromise. Rosie stiffened. 'On whose part?'

'Way to go, Rosie.' Someone in the crowd yelled. 'Make him squirm.'

Kent sent a forbidding look into the horde of his relatives.

There was muffled laughter, a couple of hoots, then silence.

'Mine,' he said softly, looking her directly in the eyes. 'I'm in love with you, O'Hanlon.'

She closed her eyes. 'Say it again.'

He bent his head toward her ear. 'I love you,' he repeated softly. 'You and the kids you want to have. I want them too.'

Her eyelids popped open. 'All the kids?'

He swallowed and set his chin as if facing into uncharted territory in hurricane force winds. 'Every last one of them.'

The assembled family clapped, cheered, and whistled.

Rosie's ragged orphan heart warmed to a toasty glow. Unable to speak, she wrapped her arms around Kent's firm waist and hugged him hard enough to crack his ribs. But there was still her future children's rival to be dealt with. She looked him in the eyes. 'And Beachline? What about it?'

196

'I spoke to Con. We've worked things out.'

'Just like that?' She was doubtful and let it show.

'No, not "just like that." We talked a long time.' He shrugged, looked confused. 'The bottom line is he wants more control and more responsibility, and I've agreed to give it to him.'

'Why?' She hoped she knew the answer but needed desperately to hear it.

He smiled and smoothed back her hair. 'Because it will give me more time to convince you how much you love me and how you can't live without me.'

Some brave soul in the crowd yelled, 'Bravo!'

Rosie shook her head. Her lower lip quivered. 'No convincing necessary. I've loved you since you strode through my door—all bad attitude and aftershave—and demanded to meet Gardenia.'

Kent took her face in his hands and kissed her. 'Thank God,' he whispered against her lips. 'Does that mean we can start over? Get things right this time?'

She looked into his eyes and smiled. 'Yes, that's exactly what it means. I'm no fool, Summerton. I know a good thing when I see it.'

He grinned.

She sobered. 'About those kids—'

This time he didn't tense up. Kent just kept

grinning, looking ridiculously pleased with himself. 'Yes?'

'I don't really want a whole, uh, dozen. I'm, uh, a bit flexible as to the exact number.' Sheesh, this compromise business was hard. 'Like maybe eight?'

He stepped back, gave her a speculative look. She could practically see that computer brain of his boot up. 'Maybe three?' he said.

'Six.'

'Four.'

'Five,' she smiled. 'And that's my best offer.'

He laughed. 'I'll take it.'

He bent his head again and murmured in her ear. His warm breath and darkly seductive voice so addled her, she didn't quite make out all the words. Something about how the sooner they got started, the better.

When she got her breath, she glanced at his family who still stood in groups at the bottom of the stairs. They seemed to be waiting for something, but she seriously doubted it was the X-rated show Kent had in mind for the two of them in her bedroom. She coughed and stepped away from him.

'Hey, Kent, can we go now?' Mike called out. He was standing near the back of the crowd holding Emma and Jane.

Kent beamed into the horde. 'Not until you all come up here, congratulate my wife-to-be, and tell her she's just made the wisest decision of her life.'

'Don't push it, dear,' his mother said, stepping up to the porch and patting his arm. 'I'll speak for all of us.' She hugged Rosie hard and kissed her cheek. 'Welcome to the family, Rosie. I always knew we were missing someone.' Another hug and she turned to the crowd. 'Now, my dear ones, move out. Let's give these two some privacy.' She smiled at Rosie. 'It's probably the last they'll ever have.'

*   *   *

Rosie, snuggled up to Kent, and watched until the last speck of dust settled back to the road. They were alone.

'Let's go inside,' Kent said.

'Let's. I'll make you something to eat. Are you hungry?'

'You could say that.' He nibbled her lobe. 'Are you? Hungry, I mean.' He kissed her throat just below her ear.

She bent her neck and sighed. 'For the same thing you are, I think. But I think I left the recipe in the bedroom.'

He'd worked his way up to kissing her cheek, the corners of her mouth. 'Then I guess we'll just have to go on up there and get it.'

He kissed her then, crushing her close, taking her mouth as if he couldn't get enough of it. The kiss was long, deep, and filled with heart. It burrowed into the deepest part of Rosie's soul.

He was hers.

She was his.

And she owed it all to some purple prose and another woman's misplaced passion.

They headed up the stairs to her bedroom. When Kent closed the door behind them, he took her back into his arms. 'What are you thinking about?'

'About you. About me. About a woman called Gardenia.'

His forehead furrowed. 'About Gardenia—'

'Forget it, Summerton. I'm not going to tell you who she is.'

'A man has ways of getting the information he wants.' He gave her a devil's grin and marched her backward toward the bed.

'Not a chance, but you're welcome to try some of those "ways" of yours. Could be fun.' The back of her knees bumped the bed and he shoved her gently backward. Propped on his elbows, he loomed over her.

'Oh, it'll be fun, O'Hanlon, I guarantee it,' he said huskily. 'And if my methods don't work tonight, I'll just have to persevere until they do. Are you ready for that?'

She smiled up at him, wound her arms around his neck, and pulled his mouth to hers. 'Ready, willing, and able,' she whispered, giving herself up to his kisses.

Before her brain hazed to a fog, a vision of love letters, Gardenia, and the 'fun' to come merged in her mind. The man of her dreams was in her arms—forever. She sighed deeply, closed her eyes, and behind his broad, strong back did a thumbs up. *I owe you, Mae.*